We hope you enjoy this book.
Please return or renew it by the due date.
You can renew it at **www.norfolk.gov.uk/libraries**
or by using our free library app. Otherwise you can
phone **0344 800 8020** - please have your library
card and pin ready.
You can sign up for email reminders too.

NORFOLK COUNTY COUNCIL
LIBRARY AND INFORMATION SERVICE

PAULA HARRISON

nosy
crow

Little
SHACKLE and
Surrounding
Area

EMBERS'
REPAIR
GARAGE

Embers
Hous

Tinder
Street

GROANING
TOR

CORNER
SHOP

Chips
Delaney's
House

BAKERY

Pebblenook
Cottage

River Kirk

First published in the UK in 2016 by Nosy Crow Ltd
The Crow's Nest, 10a Lant Street
London, SE1 1QR, UK

This edition published in 2016

Nosy Crow and associated logos are trademarks and/or registered
trademarks of Nosy Crow Ltd

Text © Paula Harrison, 2016
Cover illustration © Lisa Evans, 2016
Map and cover lettering © Sarah J Coleman, 2016

Printed and bound in the UK by Clays Ltd, St Ives Plc
Typeset by Tiger Media

Papers used by Nosy Crow are made from wood grown in
sustainable forests.

ISBN: 978 0 85763 636 2

www.nosycrow.com

For Jennie,
who explored Curbar Edge with me

Prologue

Ten years before

The little girl floated slowly downstream in the darkness, her hair rippling like water weed. She stared wide-eyed at the river surface swaying above her head. A silver minnow darted up to her. She tried to touch it but it flicked its tail and swam away. She giggled. When the fish didn't return a frown creased her forehead and she looked round for her mummy.

Bright threads of lightning zigzagged through the night sky and thunder boomed. The girl watched the shape of the lightning for a while, breathing in the deep earthy scent of the river. The water rocked her from side to side, coaxing her to close her eyes. At last, she gave in and slept.

She woke up in her father's arms. They were soaring through the dark sky. Water streamed from her dress and the cold air made her shiver.

"Daddy, I want to go home." She started to cry.

"Shh, Laney." Her dad hugged her tight. "We'll stop soon. Don't worry." He turned once to look behind.

Then he beat his wings harder, his eyes fixed on the horizon.

Patterns of lights drifted below them. Towns and villages lay undisturbed. Flat fields turned to rolling hills and then to sharp edges of rock that rose up from the ground like giants.

Laney's dad hovered for a moment, his forehead creasing. Then he swooped down over a cluster of houses and landed in front of a cottage with a red front door and creeper climbing over its weather-beaten stones. He set Laney down and knocked on the door.

Laney stared up at the round door knocker. "Daddy?"

The door opened. A man with a dark-brown beard and serious eyes stood in front of them. The sound of voices and laughter came from inside and the crackle of a fire. Laney looked in eagerly.

Laney's dad and the bearded man stared at each other for a long moment.

"She's gone, Connor," her dad croaked. "They attacked us last night. There was no warning and now she's gone."

"I knew this would happen. I told her..." The bearded man's fingers clenched around the door frame. "How did they find you?"

"I don't know. There must be spies everywhere." Her dad took a leather pouch from his pocket. His hand trembled as he gave it to the other man. "I saved her dust. She should rest here where she came from. Please – you have to do this, Connor. I daren't stay here and do it myself."

The bearded man nodded. He held the pouch awkwardly as if he didn't want to touch it.

A chill took hold of Laney's heart. "Daddy, what's that?" She tugged his arm. "I want Mummy."

The two men glanced down at her for a moment but didn't answer. "Where will you go?" said Connor.

"Better if I don't tell you," Laney's dad replied. "Then if they come to you, you'll have no secrets to hide."

"Good luck, Robert." The bearded man glanced at Laney again, briefly caressing her hair with his rough hand before he closed the door.

Laney's dad picked her up again. He looked at her steadily and his mouth twisted as if it hurt him to smile. "Mummy's gone, Laney, and we're going to find a new place to live, just you and me. You don't need to worry – I'll always look after you."

Then he spread his wings again and sped into the sky. The first rays of dawn lit up the marching bank of storm clouds behind them.

CHAPTER
1

"Dad?" Laney leaned over the hospital bed, staring at her dad's face. His eyes were shut and his forehead looked crumpled. For three and a half months she'd been watching, waiting, hoping. But he never moved. His eyes never even flickered.

Laney's stepmum, Kim, gave a sigh. "I'll have to shave his chin again. He's never liked having a beard but the nurses only get round to it once a week."

Laney felt frustration bubbling inside her. It rose up, flooding her mind. Her hands grew hotter and she hid them in her lap. "What's the point in doing that? We don't even know if he can hear us. I read him a whole book before Christmas and he did nothing."

Kim laid a hand on her arm. "The doctors said there's a chance he might be able to hear, so we have to keep trying. That's all we can do right now."

Laney looked away, her palms filled with burning heat. She knew her stepmum was trying to be nice but that made her feel worse. She couldn't stand this room – the electric monitor beeping at the end of the bed and the drip going into her dad's hand. All this was her fault. Her dad had been trying to protect her from the Shadow. He'd been trying to save her. It wasn't fair that he should be lying here unconscious just because of her.

She tried to breathe slowly. She couldn't let Kim

see what was happening to her. Secretly, she was afraid that if she let out the fire inside her then she'd lose control of it completely.

For a second, she wished she could close her eyes, change into her faerie form and fly away. She jumped up and hurried to the door. "I'm just going to the bathroom. I'll be back in a minute."

Once Laney was inside the hospital toilets, she went to the basin and let the cold water run down her wrists and over her fingers. If only she'd told her dad what she knew about the Shadow... If only she'd got back home faster that horrible day. Everything had changed so fast and now she felt like she'd lost her dad forever.

Last summer, on the night of a red full moon, Laney's magic had Awakened. She'd discovered that she belonged to a community of faeries living secretly in her village. They looked exactly like humans but they could also change into faerie form and fly. In ancient times they were known as the Fair Eyes because of the bright golden circles in their eyes.

Each faerie was part of a different tribe – Thorn, Mist, Greytail, Kestrel or Blaze – and each one had a very different kind of magic. The Thorns had power over plants and trees. The Mists, the tribe Laney's dad belonged to, could bend water to their will. The Greytails had a great affinity with animals and could understand their language. The Kestrels worked magic over the air – whipping up high winds and tornadoes. Finally, the Blaze tribe had power over fire.

Many Mists, Thorns and Greytails lived in the village of Skellmore. Each faerie's power was passed down from their parents and Laney had believed she was a Mist like her dad but she had struggled to use her magic to control water. At last she'd discovered her dad's secret. Against all the rules he'd married someone from a different tribe. Laney's mother, who had died when she was little, had been a Blaze faerie and Laney had fire magic too.

It had been a shock, but a great relief. All this time, she'd known there was something wrong with her Mist power. Many of the Skellmore faeries had watched her with suspicion for months. Awakening under a red moon – a wolf moon – was a bad sign, they had said. There was a prophecy about someone born under such a moon which spoke of disaster and destruction.

Laney had only told her closest friends, Claudia and Fletcher, that her mum had been a Blaze. Mixed-tribe marriages were forbidden in the faerie world and there were no other Blaze faeries in the village to help her learn fire magic. It seemed safer to keep it secret for now.

The cold water began to soothe the heat in

Laney's hands. Even the burn mark on her middle finger – the mark she had received the night she'd Awakened – started to feel cooler. Steam rose gently and clouded the mirror. Laney turned off the tap and wiped the glass with her sleeve, staring at her reflection and the gold rings around her pupils.

Her stepmum, Kim, was human and knew nothing about the faerie world. She couldn't even see the rings in Laney's eyes. All faeries had them but they could only be seen by other faeries. To Kim, Laney was the normal blue-eyed girl she'd always been. Yet Laney knew she had powers that would shock her stepmum. Powers that made her hands grow hot and flames burst from her palms. The fire inside her had lit when she fought the evil Shadow last autumn and now there was no going back.

Laney dried her hands and went back to her dad's room. Simon, her dad's work partner, had arrived. His arms were folded over his lanky frame and he was nodding at something Kim was saying. They both looked up as Laney came back in. Simon was leaning against the window, far away from the flowers on the bedside table, which he always said made him sneeze. His own gold-ringed eyes marked him out as another faerie and for a second Laney felt guilty that they were both keeping this secret from Kim.

"Are you all right?" Kim got up and came over to Laney. "You seem tired today."

The door opened and a doctor with silver glasses looked in. "Sorry to interrupt. Can I have a word, Mrs Rivers?"

"Of course." Kim squeezed Laney's arm and followed the doctor out of the door.

"*Are* you all right?" asked Simon, once Kim had gone.

"Fine." Laney leaned against the wall, hands in her pockets. "I guess I'm just fed up of everyone asking me that question."

"Oh, sorry." Simon looked awkward. "Well, I should ... work's busy and there's a lot to do."

Laney nodded. With her dad in here, Simon was doing the work of two people, trying to keep their plumbing business going.

Simon made his way out, nearly colliding with the door frame in an effort to avoid a nurse going past with a vase of flowers.

Once he was gone, Laney checked that no one was looking through the little square window pane in the door. Then she slipped her hand under her dad's pillow and drew out a small parcel wrapped in green cotton. Inside were dried leaves of comfrey and vervain which Gwen, a faerie Elder in the village, had said would help to bring her dad back to them. She stuffed the parcel in her jeans pocket.

She'd lost count of how many parcels of leaves they'd tried now. Nothing seemed to make any difference.

She leaned over her dad again, scanning his face. Did he even know that his family were here waiting for him?

Kim came back in, her face pale. "Did Simon leave?"

Laney nodded, her eyes still fixed on her dad.

Kim sighed. "I need to get back and collect Toby from Monique Lionhart. I don't want to leave him there for too long – he's been a bit of a handful lately."

"I know. I heard him screaming last night." Laney's little stepbrother, Toby, was only two. He didn't really understand what was going on.

"Let's go then." Kim kissed Laney's dad on the cheek.

Laney followed her stepmum out of the door. Once they'd left the hospital, she breathed more slowly. She felt awful for being glad to leave but she hated everything about that place, from the mint-green walls to the smell of disinfectant and the bottles of antibacterial gel hanging by every door.

"Laney, the doctors have suggested a plan to help your dad's recovery." Kim's voice wobbled. She fumbled in her handbag for the car keys. "They first mentioned it a couple of weeks ago but I didn't want to say anything until we knew whether there was a space."

"A space for what?" said Laney.

Kim hesitated. "The thing is, they thought he'd be a much easier case. When he first went in he was more responsive – he seemed to be able to hear people. He just didn't … improve the way they expected." She tried to smile. "But the good news is that there's a special unit for people with head injuries and they've found a space for him there. He'll be seen by doctors who are experts at treating these things."

Laney's mind whirled. "But they should've have done that weeks ago!"

"There just wasn't a space then. And they didn't want to move him at first." Kim unlocked the car and they climbed in. "The Head Injury Unit is quite a way north – in Kirkfield."

Laney's heart jolted. "How far away is that? Won't it be hard for us to see him?"

"No, because I want us to move up there too."

"What?" Laney stared.

"I was going to tell you better … somehow." Kim rubbed her forehead. "I know you have friends here and … school and things. But this unit is your dad's best hope and I don't want to be too far away from him. It'd be more than four hours' drive. This is the best way. We'll just move up there with him next week. I've already found a cottage for us to rent."

For a minute, Laney couldn't speak. Skellmore was her home. Claudia and Fletcher were here. And she had responsibilities too – an unfinished hunt for the Myricals, the objects of power that they needed to keep from the Shadow. But if this new hospital was the best thing for her dad…

"I'm sorry to tell you so suddenly." Kim broke into her thoughts. "Let's talk about it later when Toby's in bed and I'll show you the leaflet the doctors gave me."

While Kim was cooking tea, Laney shrugged her coat back on. She needed to talk to Gwen about things. Gwen Whitefern was the oldest of the Thorn tribe elders and usually gave good advice.

As she hurried down the hill into Skellmore, Laney felt her skin prickling. There was definitely tension in the air, just like the moment of stillness before a storm breaks. It probably meant there was an argument brewing between the tribes again. They had always distrusted each other but things had worsened last year when an evil Shadow faerie had begun haunting the village.

The Shadow had begun using dark spells to search for the Myricals, the sacred objects containing the essence of each tribe's magic. There were five Myricals. The Crystal Mirror belonged to the Mists. The Wildwood Arrow was owned by the

Thorns. The Vial of the Four Winds belonged to the Kestrels. The White Wolf Statue was the Greytails' and the Sparkstone belonged to the Blaze tribe. The Myricals had been lost many years before during the rise of the Great Shadow.

Laney had barely found out that she was a faerie before she was flung into a desperate race to find the Myricals. If the Shadow had found them first he would have seized each tribe's power in turn. With her friends Claudia and Fletcher, she'd saved two of them: the Crystal Mirror, belonging to the Mist tribe, and the Wildwood Arrow belonging to the Thorns. But no one knew who the Shadow was and which tribe he had come from. So now each tribe suspected the others of protecting the Shadow and the atmosphere of suspicion between them had reached breaking point.

Laney suppressed a shiver. She might have met the Shadow in human form and never realised what he really was. She remembered the last time she'd met the Shadow face to face. He had squeezed her neck with his black-gloved hand and left a thin layer of ice on her skin. Since then, she'd been convinced that the Shadow was actually a Mist – a member of her dad's tribe. Thinking of the Shadow as someone she actually knew was truly terrifying.

She passed the entrance to The Cattery – the street where the Greytails lived. Through faerie eyes, she could see their houses had animal features. Some had fur, some dark-brown spines, one even growled. At the bottom of the hill she turned into the High Street. A few people were shopping in the minimart or sitting in the hairdresser's next door. In the park opposite, the huge oak tree flushed gold with power from the faerie ring nearby. The rings were powerful gateways and were best avoided unless you wanted to be sucked into the Otherworld beyond. Laney wondered if ordinary people ever sensed all this magic that they couldn't see.

Gnarlwood Lane was quiet as usual. The Thorns lived here and the whole street was filled with Thorn magic. Old Mr Willowby, an elderly Thorn man, was out in his front garden, raking up fallen leaves. Laney ran up to Gwen's house with its white flower roof and rapped on the front door.

Gwen opened the door. A purple hat with sprigs of lavender was perched on her white curls. "Hello, Laney. Come in." She stepped back to let Laney inside. "How are you? Is there any improvement in your father?"

"Not really," Laney sighed. "I'm still trying your herbs." She took the small parcel of dried leaves wrapped in green cotton out of her jeans pocket and handed it to Gwen.

"It's odd – I've haven't seen an injury so hard to treat for a long time," Gwen muttered. "There may be something we haven't tried. I will consult with the other Thorn Elders."

Laney knitted her fingers together. "There might not be time for that. My dad's getting transferred to a special hospital."

"Indeed." Gwen looked thoughtful. "Where's that?"

"It's in Kirkfield. Kim says that's up north. She told me about it just now. There's a special place that treats head injuries and that's where they're sending him." Laney twisted her fingers together. The thought of leaving Skellmore was awful, but if that's what her dad needed...

"Perhaps it's not entirely a bad thing for your father to be taken away from Skellmore," said Gwen. "If the danger from the Shadow grows then he'll be safer away from it all."

Laney sat down on Gwen's sofa. She remembered the moment her dad had faced the Shadow faerie. Red lightning had blasted from the Shadow's fingers, striking him in the chest and knocking him to the ground. He had hit his head as he fell. She closed her eyes, trying to banish the picture from her mind, but it wouldn't go away. She took a deep breath. "The thing is, Kim wants us all to move up there. I can't help find the next Myrical if I'm so far away. There are still three more of them to find and the Shadow will be looking for them too."

Gwen, who had begun watering a plant on the window sill, set down the little watering can and looked at Laney sharply. The curling silver marks of an Elder gleamed on the back of her hands. "We discussed this before. You and Fletcher and Claudia need to leave the Myrical search to the Elders now. Our kin from the Blaze and Kestrel tribes in the north and west know what's happening and each tribe is making its own arrangements. They're looking for the Shadow too. These are dangerous times. You are *not* to get involved."

Laney's hands grew hot and she hid them behind her back. "A few months ago nobody else believed there was a Shadow faerie at all! Claudia, Fletcher and I found the Crystal Mirror and the Wildwood Arrow. I want to help beat the Shadow. I would have spent more time searching but it's been hard with my dad ill."

Gwen frowned. "Maybe it would be good for you to get away from Skellmore too. I know you're having trouble hiding your abilities. Everyone believes you to be a Mist faerie like your father. If they see you using Blaze powers then life will become very difficult for you here."

Laney flushed. Gwen was the only person, apart from her friends Fletcher and Claudia, who knew about her Blaze powers. The Thorn Elder had guessed her secret after the Shadow's last attack.

Luckily she'd agreed that Laney's magic should be kept secret for now.

"I am trying to do better! It's just that my Blaze magic's new and sometimes I forget … but I will keep it hidden."

"Are you sure that you can?" Gwen's gaze was fixed on Laney's face. "Blaze power – bending fire to your will – is the most dangerous and unpredictable of all the faerie powers. I've been concerned for some time that you are not learning to control it."

"It's not easy to find a place away from everyone where I can practise. I should go. Kim will start wondering where I am." Laney pushed herself up off the sofa, leaving black marks on its flowery cover as her hands scorched the fabric. A smell of burning filled the air.

"Laney!" Gwen exclaimed.

"I'm sorry! I didn't mean to—" Laney backed to the door, trying not to touch anything else, but a tiny flame burst from her between her fingers.

"Laney, wait a minute. There's no need to go like this."

"I have to. Kim's cooking tea." Laney managed to push down the latch with her elbow. She got the door open and rushed outside. How could Gwen say that it would be better if she went away? Skellmore was her home. It was everything she knew.

Her hands burned again and a puff of flame burst

upwards, scorching the branch of a tree right above her. The wood blackened and the branch broke in two, crashing on to the path below. Laney looked back at Gwen, who was standing in the doorway. Then she ran off down the road.

The heat in Laney's hands faded as she ran. She shouldn't have gone to Gwen's house. Gwen didn't understand how she was feeling at all. There was no one else in Skellmore like her. There were Thorns who'd married other Thorns. Or Mists who'd married other Mists. That was the way it was. You stayed with your tribe and powers were passed down from parents to children.

But not for her.

Her Mist tribe dad, Robert Rivers, had married a Blaze faerie – Cordelia Embers. Water had married fire.

Laney didn't know what had happened next. She only knew her mum had died when she was little and after that her dad had moved to Skellmore and hidden the truth from everyone. There wasn't a single faerie she'd met whose parents had married outside their tribe. She wished there was another Blaze living in Skellmore. Was it normal for the flames to appear in her hands so easily? Was there a way to control the fire? There was no one to ask.

She sped up, suddenly aware of other people in the street. Mr Willowby was still in his garden but she didn't think he'd noticed the flame in her hand. He was sitting on his front step and he didn't look up or wave as she went by. Laney turned on to the High Street. A bus drew up by the minimart. Her friend, Claudia Lionhart, leapt off with cat-like grace, her dark hair swinging over her shoulders. Her mum climbed off after her and Laney tried to catch up with them.

Then a terrible scream made her heart jump.

People looked round, startled. Laney was sure the cry had come from behind her – from Gnarlwood Lane. She spun round and dashed back the way she'd come. The cry sounded high, like a child or a woman. She stopped at the Willowbys' garden. Mr Willowby was lying on his side on the front step and clutching one arm to his chest while the other hung loosely.

His wife was leaning over him, her face contorted. "Someone quickly – help me!"

Laney hesitated but, before she could decide what to do, Fletcher's dad, Mr Thornbeam, pushed past her and ran up the path. "What happened? Did he have an accident?" He lifted Mr Willowby's arm to take his pulse.

"I think it's his heart," Mrs Willowby sobbed. "He hasn't been feeling well for days."

"Shall I call an ambulance?" Laney asked them.

"No!" Mr Thornbeam replied sharply. "Find Gwen."

Laney turned to follow his instruction but Gwen was already coming down the lane. Claudia and her mum came up behind her from the direction of the High Street.

"What happened?" said Claudia.

Claudia's mum, a small woman with huge energy, took in the situation with one quick glance. "Quickly, Claudia! We have to make sure that no humans come down here."

"What? How?" Claudia said.

Mrs Lionhart was already rushing back to the entrance of the lane. "Tell them there's a gas leak. That'll do it."

While Claudia and her mum guarded the road entrance, Gwen leaned over Mr Willowby. She spoke under her breath. Laney edged closer, watching in horrified fascination.

A faint shimmer gathered around Mr Willowby's body like sunlight glistening on the surface of a lake. Mrs Willowby's shoulders began to shake. "Don't go," she repeated. "Don't go…"

Mr Thornbeam put an arm around her.

Gwen stepped back a little. "I'm sorry, Millie. There's nothing I can do."

The glow around Mr Willowby grew brighter. Laney thought he looked like an angel and for a moment she couldn't breathe. Then, with a sudden flash, his body and the light were gone and all that was left on the front step was a small heap of grey dust.

Silence fell on Gnarlwood Lane. No one moved.

Mr Thornbeam said in a low voice. "We need to

collect his dust and keep it safe, Millie. Do you have something suitable?"

Mrs Willowby's shoulders were still shaking.

"I'll fetch something," Gwen told them.

Laney didn't move. She was mesmerised by the heap of dust on the front doorstep. That was all that was left of Mr Willowby. Just dust. Faerie dust.

A group of faeries were gathering around the edge of the Willowbys' garden. They stood silently, each tribe separate from the others. Laney noticed that her friend Fletcher was there too, standing with the other Thorns.

Gwen returned with a small purse embroidered with snowdrops. Mrs Willowby took it and, with a wave of her fingers, drew her husband's dust into the pouch before closing it tight. Then she looked across at the Thorns, gathered just beyond the garden gate.

The Thorns linked hands, and a circle of roses grew around Mrs Willowby. Rising higher, they burst into bloom and filled the air with a sweet scent. The Mists stepped forward next and a light rain fell, leaving water gleaming on the flower petals. Lastly, the Greytails whispered to each other. Then Claudia gave a long piercing whistle and three white doves fluttered down to land by the rose circle.

Mrs Willowby clasped the purse tightly and blinked back tears. "Thank you, everyone. My husband was a kind man. He … he believed in peace and he wanted fighting between the tribes to stop."

The sky darkened. Laney shivered and glanced up at a black cloud that had drifted in from the south.

"We've lived in Skellmore for forty-five years," Mrs Willowby said chokingly. "They were happy years."

People behind Laney began muttering to each other. She folded her arms over her chest. Why was it suddenly so cold?

Mrs Willowby tailed off and stared at the thickening black cloud. A shower of hail poured down, pelting the roses with ice. The doves flew off in alarm.

Suddenly Laney knew what was coming. "It's the Shadow!" she yelled.

"Stay where you are, all of you," Gwen ordered, but the rest of her words were lost as everyone scattered.

"Laney!" Claudia pulled her arm. "We've got to get out of here."

Suddenly, Laney understood. The Shadow would be coming for the dust. That was why everyone was afraid. She looked at their stricken faces and a sick feeling rose inside her. Everyone knew exactly why the Shadow wanted Mr Willowby's dust. That was how Shadow magic worked – the remains of a dead faerie were used to work the dark spells.

Mrs Willowby was still standing inside the circle of ruined flowers, holding the purse with her husband's dust to her chest. The wind whipped round her, beating her grey hair.

Gwen and the other Elders ushered her into the house, before following her in and shutting the door. The wind strengthened and hail fell in jagged pieces like broken glass. Claudia let go of Laney's arm and stumbled away, shielding her face.

There was a growl of thunder and Laney glimpsed the thing she still saw in every nightmare.

Red lightning.

A jagged lightning bolt struck the tree beside Fletcher. The tree groaned and a branch broke away, striking him as it fell.

"Fletcher!" Laney grabbed his arm and pulled him down the street.

Something dark swooped behind the rooftops, just out of sight. The hail grew faster until thick balls of ice covered the road. Laney and Fletcher hid behind a hedge. Laney scanned the sky for the Shadow.

"That monster's after the dust." Fletcher clenched his fists. "I have to get back there!"

"It's too dangerous!" Laney said quickly. The last time they'd faced the Shadow she'd nearly lost Fletcher completely. The dark faerie had been searching for the Wildwood Arrow, which was sacred to Thorns like Fletcher, and all of Skellmore had been overcome by an evil enchantment.

As the hail slowed, the Willowbys' front door opened and Lucas Frogley rushed out followed by Mr Thornbeam and the other Elders. From inside the house came the sound of weeping.

"Dad!" Fletcher called.

Mr Thornbeam's face was grim. "Go home, son," he said. "Make sure that your sister and your mother are all right."

"What happened?" said Fletcher.

Mr Thornbeam paused before he answered. "I don't know how he did it – the whole place went pitch black. But he got in and Willowby's dust is gone."

Fletcher swore under his breath.

Lucas Frogley, the tribe leader, scowled at Laney and the expression on his pale, bony face said it all. He didn't trust her. When she'd first Awakened, Laney had believed she was a Mist faerie because her dad was. None of the adults except Gwen knew the truth about her Blaze mum. If Frogley found out, he would trust her even less.

Laney looked up, expecting to see more red lightning flickering overhead, but the clouds had faded and were drifting away from Skellmore.

The Shadow had struck and then vanished.

CHAPTER 3

Lightning split the sky that night. Laney was woken by the sound of thunder and watched it from her bedroom window. The storm appeared at intervals – first above Hobbin Forest and then to the south over Skellmore Edge. But there was no red lightning – so where was the Shadow? And what spell would he make with Mr Willowby's dust? She shivered.

To make herself feel better, she took a book from her bedside table. It was *The Wind in the Willows* and her mum's name, Cordelia Embers, was written in the front in childish round handwriting. She'd found it among her dad's things after he was hurt last autumn. It was the only thing of her mum's that she had.

When she went downstairs the next morning, Kim was talking to Simon in the kitchen. Laney heard her name mentioned and hung back to listen.

"What else am I supposed to do, Simon?" Kim said. "I need to be close to Robert. I know it's hard on the kids having to move but we'll keep our house here, of course." There was a snap as a cupboard door closed.

"You don't need to move there to see Robert," Simon replied. "I'll drive you up to visit him every week. You don't have to cope with all this alone."

"That's a really kind offer," Kim said, "but I couldn't let you do that. I know how busy you are with work now that you're doing it all on your own."

"I'm happy to help. I've known Robert ever since he moved here and that's more than ten years ago. You're like family, really."

Laney edged closer to the kitchen door, wondering what Kim would say. Her stepmum's voice was firm. "It's really kind but I've thought about travelling up to visit and I just can't see it working. The kids would spend half their lives in the car."

Laney walked into the kitchen and leaned against the table.

"Morning, love." Kim smiled at her. "Did you sleep OK? There was such a storm last night."

Laney didn't want to talk about the storm. "I heard you talking about moving. What's going to happen about my school?"

Kim took a deep breath. "I know this is all really sudden for you but I've had some time to think about it. I've found you a school in Kirkfield and I've found a cottage we can rent in a village nearby – a place called Little Shackle."

Laney clasped her hands tightly, suddenly afraid she would lose control and burn something. "You've already found a house and a school! I'm not even sure I want to go. All my friends are here. Everything's here!"

"Come and sit down a minute." Kim drew out two chairs. She put her hand on Laney's arm. "I know this feels really sudden. I'm sorry to spring it on you. But I didn't want to say anything before because none of it was certain until the doctors found a bed for your dad in the Head Injury Unit. I've found us a nice place to stay – a little cottage near some hills. I've only seen it in the agent's photos but it looks lovely."

Simon drank from his coffee mug, leaning against the kitchen worktop.

"Why can't we drive up there like Simon said?" asked Laney. "Why do we have to stay?"

"It's such a long drive and I think we need to be close by. What if your dad's condition changes? You know it would be awful to be far away if something happened. Or maybe he'll start to respond to us. Then we'll be able to help a bit more." Kim smiled.

Laney's heart ached. She wanted so badly to believe that her dad would be better soon. Maybe this new hospital would make a real difference. If her dad woke up she wanted to be there. And what if Gwen was right about him being safer away from Skellmore? Kim and Toby would be safer too. What happened yesterday showed that the Shadow was still watching the village. "OK," she said, "let's go. As soon as dad gets better we can come back here, right?"

"That's right!" Kim reached up and smoothed a curl away from Laney's face.

"So, how soon do we leave?" Laney asked.

"The lease for the cottage starts at the weekend," Kim told her. "We can go as soon as we're packed."

"Don't you think you're rushing into this?" Simon broke in. "It might be better to take some time and work out what you want to do."

"There's no point in waiting," Kim said, her voice rising. "We need to go."

Toby ran in. "Mummy, I seen a cat! I seen a cat!"

"Where's the cat, honey?" said Kim, scooping him up.

Laney took this opportunity to slip out of the back door. She needed time to think. Following her instinct, she turned left down Beacon Way and followed the footpath out of Skellmore. She crossed a stile and walked across the fields leading up to Skellmore Edge, the flat rocky outcrop that towered over the village. By the time she got to the top she was out of breath.

Skellmore was spread out like a tiny model village with the shining ribbon of the Mistray River lying across the topmost corner. Leaving the place would be really weird. She'd lived here nearly all her life – all the bits she could remember properly. She only recalled tiny broken details of the early years before her mum died and those memories seemed too strange and sketchy to rely on.

She watched a bird of prey circling over a field

below. In the bright sunshine, the danger from the Shadow seemed less real. She tried to imagine those fields turning black, the green shoots of corn turning to ash...

A small dark shape twined around her ankle, making her jump. "Dizzy! What are you doing here?"

The cat gazed back with bright-green eyes.

"She told me where you were." Claudia leapt from one rock to another and reached the smooth flat hilltop. "I want to talk to you."

"You know sneaking up on people is really annoying."

Claudia grinned. "I can't help it – it's a Greytail thing. Actually I hardly bothered to be quiet. You were basically daydreaming – I'd have had to stomp up here like a Thorn to get your attention."

Laney jerked her head at the village. "What's going on down there?"

"Bad stuff." Claudia pushed her dark hair over her shoulder and stretched out on a flat bit of rock. Her cat, Dizzy, lay down next to her. "You saw the lightning last night, right? The Elders had sent people out to guard the village. Then Thorns ran into Mists and Mists ran into Greytails and they all panicked."

Laney sat down too. "So they fought each other instead of the Shadow?"

"Typical, huh? The Thorns are the worst. They're sooo trigger-happy right now. I can't believe I'm saying this, but I miss the way they used to be – all dull and boring and *let's grow some cabbage.*"

"I know what you mean." Laney curled her hair round her finger. She couldn't believe she'd be leaving this place soon.

"Laney?" Claudia clicked her fingers in front of Laney's face. "So tell me where you're moving to. When does Kim want to leave?"

"Hey! How do you know about that?"

"My mum saw Kim in the estate agent's in Pennington last week and Dizzy was hanging round your back door this morning and told me a bit of what you were talking about."

"Dizzy, you spy!" Laney glared at the cat.

Dizzy turned her back and started washing her face with her paws.

"Kim only told me yesterday." Laney explained about her dad being taken to the hospital in Kirkfield and Kim finding them a cottage to rent.

"You should go," said Claudia as soon as she'd finished. "Seriously, you should. Lots of the Blaze tribe live up there, that's what my mum says, and you could learn Blaze skills from them."

Laney looked at her friend in horror. "What have you been saying to your mum?"

"Don't panic! I haven't told her anything. I

know how to keep a secret. We were talking about Kirkfield because my aunt lives there with millions of my cousins."

"So there are Greytails there?"

"Uh-huh! We get everywhere." Claudia grinned. "I'd better go actually. I'm meant to be practising defence spells with Tom." She made a face.

Laney laughed. Tom was Claudia's older brother and the two of them always argued. She stayed up on the Edge for a while after Claudia left, looking at Skellmore and thinking about everything. Turning her hands palm up, she wished for fire. Small flames surged from her palms. They were beautiful – reddish-orange around the edge and golden in the centre. She focused her mind, trying to keep the flames small without putting them out. Where did the fire come from? Had her mother ever sat by herself practising this exact same thing?

She managed to keep the flames burning evenly for a few minutes before one of them leapt into the air and the other one died.

Then she brushed the dust off her jeans and made her way back down the hill to Skellmore.

The day before they left, Laney was in the living room packing up the last of their things. She'd filled two boxes with books, leaving the bookcase empty apart from a blue shoebox on the top shelf. Taking the box down, she couldn't resist taking a look at the papers and old photos inside. Near the top was a picture of Laney's mum holding Laney when she was a baby.

Kim came in with more packing crates. "What's in there? Oh, Laney, you look so cute!"

"Thanks!" Laney smiled. It was her favourite picture of her mum, taken in the garden at their old house. Her mum was standing in front of a tree with bare branches and there was a grey, wintry sky in the background.

"Look at you! You're so tiny." Kim took the photo for a closer look. "You must have only been a few days old in that picture. Babies don't stay that small for very long."

"I don't remember our old garden at all so I must have been pretty young when we left." Laney gazed at the tree in the picture.

Kim put the photo back in the shoebox. "I'd better carry on. I want to pack a bit more before I start dinner." She smiled at Laney and went upstairs.

Laney put the lid on the shoebox and packed it into the crate. She frowned. Something was wrong – something important. What was it?

She glanced at the shoebox and a strange impulse made her take the lid off and study the photo again. It was the tree that seemed odd, she realised. It had completely bare branches and that meant it must have been winter. The bushes at the edge of the picture were bare too.

Laney pushed back a wisp of hair and tried to get her thoughts straight. Kim had said she must have been only a few days old in this photo but her birthday was 15th July, so why did it look like winter?

A worried feeling wriggled inside her. She tipped the things out of the shoebox and looked for other clues. There were more photos of her mum and her as a newborn baby, each one with wintry trees in the background. Then, tucked inside a torn envelope, she found a card decorated with flowers which read *Thinking of You*. Inside there was a message to Robert and Cordelia, her mum and dad.

To Cordelia and Robert,

We're thinking of you at this difficult time. We hope baby Laney is doing well and congratulations on having a little girl. Hope to see you soon,

Love from all of us xxx

Laney read the message again. The card must have been sent after she was born, but why had it been a difficult time? She turned the envelope over to check if there was a postmark. When she saw it she could hardly breathe: *Kirkfield 9th February*.

Then maybe she hadn't been born on the 15th July. All these years she'd been celebrating her birthday on that day. No wonder her dad had always seemed a little strange about it. He would have been the one that changed things, the one that kept the secret about the date of her real birthday. And she could guess exactly why he'd done it.

When she'd first Awakened as a faerie, the tribe Elders had been suspicious of her. There'd been so many strange things – the way she hadn't Awakened until twelve years old and the way her Mist powers had never seemed to work. They'd asked her dad whether she was born on the night of a red moon. This was meant to be a bad sign because of an ancient prophecy.

Checking that Kim wasn't around, Laney switched on the computer and searched the Internet for dates that red moons had occurred. There was only one in the year she was born: 9th February.

So this was it – the last secret that her dad had kept from her. She had been born on the night of a red moon after all. The words of the prophecy started running through her head:

Born under a Wolf Moon
The Child of Aether joins together powers far apart.
He binds the opposites

And drives a splinter through the faerie ring's heart.

It couldn't mean her, could it? She rubbed her aching forehead. Those lines in the middle … *joins together powers far apart … binds the opposites*. Fire and water were opposites and those were the two types of faerie magic she knew. Fire from her mum and water from her dad.

What was a Child of Aether anyway? Laney sighed. None of it made any sense. But there was one thing she knew for sure: her dad wouldn't have hidden her real birthday unless he'd thought he had to. She'd seen enough of the tribes, especially the Mists with Frogley as their leader, to know she shouldn't tell lots of people what she'd discovered. She wanted to tell Claudia and Fletcher, but there was little time before she left tomorrow.

She typed *Child of Aether* into the Internet search but it just came up with lots of scientific words. There was something about chemicals and flammable liquids – but she didn't understand it.

Laney bit her lip. It was hard trying to take everything in. She'd been born on the 9th February – that meant she was nearly thirteen already!

She piled everything back into the shoebox and put on the lid. She would keep this to herself until she'd had time to figure out what it all meant. Her stomach did a somersault as she thought of the move tomorrow. The postmark on the letter had read Kirkfield. That was where her dad's new hospital was. Maybe the card had come from a Blaze faerie – a friend of her mum's. Maybe she would meet some other Blaze faeries and discover more about the fire magic inside her.

CHAPTER

4

Claudia and Fletcher came to see Laney off the next morning. Claudia promised she'd try to visit the next time her family went to visit her aunt in Kirkfield.

Laney watched the houses flick past the car window as they drove out of Skellmore. Mist houses with their shimmering watery colours, the creature-like Greytail homes and the Thorn houses with their tree-bark walls and leafy roofs. She would miss everything – even the gigantic green cat eyes that stared at her from the wall of the Lionhart Pet Shop. She would miss it all.

After a few hours, they came off the motorway and took a winding road through the hills. Villages rolled by with houses all made from the same mottled brown stone. Thoughts spun round Laney's head like crows circling a tree. What would she say if she met another Blaze faerie? Would she know they were the same tribe right away? Would they think it was strange that she didn't know any Blaze spells? A knot of excitement grew in her stomach. This could be her chance to find out where she really belonged.

At last, Kim pulled over and stopped the car. She smiled at Laney and Toby. "Here we are!"

Laney got out and stretched her aching legs. The house was small and made from the same worn brown stone as the other houses she'd seen. A name plaque on the door read Pebblenook Cottage. A magpie watched them intently from the top of the mossy roof. It hopped down to the corner of the house, then stopped and tilted its head sideways.

Laney stared back. The bird gave a loud "*Caw!*" and flew off, white flashing against black as it flapped its wings.

"Caw!" repeated Toby, and he climbed up on the rickety garden gate and swung back and forth.

The garden was overgrown and there was a crooked tree that was just coming into blossom.

"Let's go inside, shall we?" Kim said. "Where have I put the key?"

"So you're the new 'uns!" A round-cheeked woman looked across the fence from next door. "Have you come far? Are you staying long?"

"I..." Kim fumbled in her handbag.

"If you can't find your key, dear, just use the spare one. It's always kept under the flowerpot on the left," said the woman. "I'm Mrs McKee, by the way, and you must be Mrs Rivers. We're neighbours now. I'm looking forward to getting to know you all. Is there a Mr Rivers?"

Flushing, Kim fished the key out from under the flowerpot. "My husband's not very well actually. Anyway, it was nice to meet you." She turned the key in the lock and steered Laney and Toby inside, shutting the door behind them.

Laney looked round the dark hallway. She flicked a light switch but it didn't work.

"It's probably just a fuse that needs changing," Kim told her. "I'll sort it out and then what we need is a nice cup of tea. Laney, could you run down to the shops and get us some milk? Just follow the road down to the village. I'm sure there'll be somewhere on the main street that you can buy it from." She handed Laney a five-pound note.

"OK, I won't be long." Laney noticed the dark rings under Kim's eyes as she hugged her. "Maybe the shop will have cake."

"Maybe," Kim said, laughing. "Any treat would be nice!"

Leaving the cottage, Laney followed the road downhill. She could already see the village lying in a hollow at the bottom of the valley. A bank of hills circled the village and sheep were scattered across the lower slopes. The tallest hill was crowned with white rock that gleamed in the afternoon sunshine. Rough boulders dotted the hillside below.

Laney made her way down the road and crossed a humpback bridge with a stream running beneath it. A signpost read *Little Shackle* in chipped black letters.

Everyone she passed on the street looked at Laney curiously, as if they knew she was a stranger.

But none of them had gold-ringed eyes. There was a church, a pub and a bakery with a delicious baking smell drifting through its open doorway. At the end of the street, there was a corner shop selling milk, tins of soup and a mix of other things. Laney bought milk, ginger cake and a little plastic T-Rex toy for Toby. She was leaving the shop when she caught sight of a strange-looking house further down on the other side of the road. Her stomach flipped over.

The house glowed like fire. It had a red front door. Orange flames rippled up the brickwork and flickered into yellow at the top. There was no smoke – the house wasn't actually alight, Laney realised. It was simply decorated with signs of magic.

It had to be a Blaze house. It just had to be.

She went closer, the shopping bag banging against her legs. Her hands grew warm and her heart began to race. She'd never met any Blazes. How should she introduce herself? What if they didn't like her?

The red door was flung open and a boy with curly black hair and glasses came out. Laney drew back, suddenly panicked. Maybe she should come back when she'd thought about what to say. Her heart skipping, she ran back up the hill to the cottage.

Kim told Laney she didn't have to start her new school till the following Monday, which suited

Laney fine. Her dad had been transferred to the Head Injury Unit in Kirkfield Hospital. The unit was a small building, separate from the main hospital, with large, comfortable rooms.

"He doesn't look so pale any more," Laney told Kim the first time they went to visit him.

"I was thinking that too." Kim sounded teary. She smiled and hugged Laney. "The doctors told me they're going to begin by adjusting his medication. This place could be just what he needs."

The cottage was warm and cosy, and once their boxes were unpacked Laney found she really liked the place. Kim said it would be nice to have a fire in the fireplace and Laney waited till she wasn't looking before trying to light the coals with her hands. A spear-like flame burst straight up the chimney and Laney had to work hard to get it under control. Once the coals were burning steadily, she sat back and stared into the flickering flames. She would never in a million years have been allowed to do this back in Skellmore. Her dad had banned all matches, candles and anything that burned. She still didn't know why. There was so much she wanted to ask him.

On Saturday afternoon, Laney felt restless. The February wind was tearing up the valley and howling round the cottage. "I'm going out for a bit," she called to Kim.

Pulling on her coat, she walked down the road to Little Shackle and scanned the ring of hills that surrounded the village. Which way should she go? There were two spots that looked interesting but they were on opposite sides of the valley. On the left was the tallest hill – a pale rocky peak pointing to the sky. On the right, the line of hills was slashed apart by a deep ravine and there was mist rising from the gap.

Laney decided to climb the tallest peak and took a left turn out of Little Shackle. The path branched away from the road and she followed it. A stile took her over the dry stone wall into a field full of sheep. She weaved past clumps of thick, spear-like grass and climbed rough boulders embedded into the hillside. Her eyes were drawn to the stony peak. She felt almost as if it was pulling her in. The path grew rockier and steeper and she scrambled up the last few metres to a stretch of flat rock just below the summit.

The wind buffeted round her, rushing in her ears. She gazed at the rumpled spread of fields and farmhouses below. It was amazing to be up here on top of the world – almost as good as flying. She hadn't dared to go flying at night here yet but she was sure it would be amazing. She imagined switching to faerie form, leaping into the air and swooping down the valley with the breeze streaming over her wings. The worries of Skellmore – the evil Shadow and the hunt for the Myricals – all seemed so far away.

She clambered on to a boulder and sat down. The rock felt gritty and crumbs of white glinted on the mottled surface. A bird rose shrieking from the undergrowth and flew down the valley. The village of Little Shackle looked tiny but even from here she could see the signs of faerie houses. There were two roads that belonged to the tribes – one was a Blaze street and the other was full of Greytail houses. There were no signs of Mists, Thorns or Kestrels in the village at all. Soon she would go and speak to the other Blazes – once she'd decided what she should say.

Scrambling up, she took the last few steps to the top of the pale, rocky peak. Strangely, there was a crack in the summit that opened into a deep, dark hole. She peered down and for a second she thought she saw a glimmer of orange at the bottom.

"What are you doing?" Someone sprang out from behind a boulder. It was the boy with curly black hair that she'd seen the day they arrived, coming out of a Blaze house. Despite the cold, he was only wearing jeans and a black T-shirt. Gold-ringed eyes glinted behind his glasses.

"I wanted to see the view from the top." Laney

pushed her windswept hair out of her face. "I've just moved here."

"This is Groaning Tor." The boy glared. "It's Blaze territory and you're trespassing."

"Are you serious? It's a hill with some sheep! Anyway I'm a Blaze too so I can't be trespassing."

"Don't lie! You're a Mist," said the boy.

Laney noticed he said it the exact same way he might say, "*you're a thief.*" She felt her palms start to burn and automatically closed her fingers. How could he have thought she was a Mist? Couldn't he see the Blaze power in her? Well, at least she didn't have to hide it here. Holding out one hand, she concentrated on the flame. "If I'm a Mist, how come I can do this?"

The boy's eyebrows lifted and for a second he seemed less sure of himself. "Well, you *look* like a Mist. Or maybe it's just because you're from the south."

Laney felt a flash of anger and the flame in her hand burned higher. "So sorry to be standing on *your* hill," she snapped. "Do any more of the hills belong to you? If I know which ones, I can keep away from them."

The boy frowned, ignoring her comment. "Are you the one who's moved into Pebblenook Cottage? I saw a lady with a little boy in the shop this morning but she wasn't a faerie."

"That was my stepmum and Toby. Yes, we've just moved into the cottage." Laney took a deep breath. She wished she hadn't snapped at him. This wasn't how she'd wanted her first meeting with another Blaze to go. "I'm Laney, by the way. So are there many Blazes living in Little Shackle? My friend, Claudia, said there would be. Have you lived here all your life? Do you train to be a Blaze and practise spells together?"

The boy's frown deepened. "Look, I can't tell you things about my tribe without knowing who you are. If you really belong to the Blaze tribe you need to go to see the Elder straightaway. That's the rule."

Laney could feel her blood thumping in her ears. She tried to keep a grip on her temper. "I'm only asking how many Blazes there are. Why are you being so weird about it?"

"You're the one that's weird!" The boy's eyes glinted. "You can make fire but you don't look like a Blaze, not really, and then you ask all these questions. I'm not giving lots of information away. There's talk of a Shadow down south – that's what they say!"

Laney's skin prickled at the mention of the Shadow. It was obvious this boy wasn't going to help her. "Fine, don't tell me anything! I'll ask someone else." She marched back down the slope.

Climbing over a stile at the bottom, she found

herself in a different road than before. Glancing back she could see the Blaze boy still watching her so she carried on trying to look like she knew where she was going. Why had she lost her temper like that? Ever since she'd found her Blaze power there'd been this fire burning inside her. Sometimes it was so hard stopping it from bursting out.

A light drizzle began to fall as she reached the first house on the street. She walked on, scanning the houses for signs of faerie magic. The only place that looked different was a huge house cut off by a high wall and big iron gates. For a second Laney thought she saw firelight playing across the walls but when she looked again it was gone. Pulling up her hood to keep off the rain, she carried on walking.

A loud banging was coming from the shop on the corner. Laney looked in, realising it was a repair garage. Black tarmac covered the front yard and a shiny black motorbike was parked in the middle. Lights were on inside the workshop and the building next door had a red frontage with the words *Embers' Repairs* painted on the window.

Laney's heart jumped painfully and she stared at the words painted on the glass.

Embers' Repairs.

Embers had been her mum's name. Was it possible these people had known her mum? She remembered the postmark on that envelope she'd found from years ago, which had said Kirkfield. Maybe her mum's family and friends still lived in this area.

A cold shakiness filled her chest and she tried to ignore it. She had to find out who they were and if they'd ever known someone called Cordelia Embers.

"Hello?" She edged closer to the workshop. There was no answer from inside. A car was raised up on a jack and piles of tools lay on a workbench. A few tyres were propped up against the back wall.

Laney turned, deciding to try the building next door. She ran her hand over the wet leather seat of the motorbike in the yard.

"What are you doing?"

It was the dark-haired boy again. "None of your business," she told him. "Are you following me or something?"

The shop door opened and a man in black overalls came out. He had a dark bristly beard, a lined face and gold-ringed eyes. He stared at her before turning to the boy. "What's going on, Tyler?"

The boy jerked his head at her. "It's this girl, Dad. I met her on top of Groaning Tor and she says she's a Blaze but she doesn't look like one. Now she's here, messing with your bike."

Laney pulled her hand off the seat of the motorbike. "I wasn't messing with it. I just wanted to stop and ask something…" She trailed off. She didn't really want to ask about the Embers name in front of this boy.

"Ask what?" Suspicion crept into the man's eyes. "You're not old enough to ride that. I don't sell bikes to ten-year-olds."

"I'm thirteen," said Laney. "It's not about the bike anyway. I just … I saw the name of your shop. I knew someone called Embers and I was going to ask if you knew them too."

"She was asking weird questions before too," Tyler told his dad. "Shall I get the Elder?"

"No!" The man's face changed and he stared at Laney as if she might disappear. "Go back home, Tyler. Right now."

Tyler said something under his breath but he did as he was told. Frowning at Laney, he stuck his hands in his pockets and walked off down the street.

"Who did you know called Embers?" The man stepped closer and Laney could smell the engine oil on his overalls.

"It was my mum," Laney said. "But she died when I was little." A sudden memory bubbled up in her mind. *A dark night… A cottage with a red front door…*

The man dropped his voice. "Are you Elaine? Tell me quickly."

It took Laney a moment to understand. "I'm Laney. No one calls me Elaine, except my dad."

The man glanced up and down the street before holding the shop door open. "You'd better come in."

Laney followed him past the front counter and down a passage. There was a small kitchen at the back with a table and chairs. The man pulled out a chair for her and leaned against the worktop, folding his huge arms.

Laney sat down. Her heart was racing and yet there was something so reassuring about this man. Something solid.

"Where's your dad?" he said, "Is he with you?"

Laney shook her head, a lump forming in her throat. It was hard explaining to people that her dad was ill – it brought all the sadness back.

The man rubbed his beard, his gold eyes thoughtful. "Then how did you know where to come?"

"I didn't. But I knew my mum's name was Embers before she was married and…" She paused, searching his face. "Did you know her? She was Cordelia Embers."

The man smiled for the first time. "Cordelia was my little sister. I'm Connor Embers – your uncle."

CHAPTER

5

Laney smiled back. She hadn't known that her mum had had a brother!

"The last time I saw you was the night Cordelia died," said Mr Embers. "That must have been at least ten years ago. You still have the same look about you. That Mist look. Comes from your dad, I suppose."

Laney flushed. "I'm not a Mist, though—"

Her uncle held up a hand to silence her. Laney heard the clunk of the door and a voice called, "Hey, Connor! There's a breakdown on Cowton Lane – an old chap in a clapped-out diesel."

"I'll be right with you," her uncle called back, before saying quietly to Laney, "Come to my house tonight. It's number seven Tinder Street. Come after dark." Then he was striding away down the passage.

Laney smiled to herself as the door closed behind him. She had an uncle she'd never known about – her mum's brother! He'd be able to tell her more about her mum as a little girl – what sort of things she liked and where they used to play. There were so many things she wanted to know.

But what about the boy – Tyler? If Mr Embers was her uncle, he must be her cousin. Why did she have to lose her temper with him like that? He hadn't exactly been easy to talk to but maybe he would be nicer now he knew they were family.

The rain stopped as she left the repair shop. Mist began rolling down the hills into Little Shackle like surf rolling on to a beach. Laney twisted a tendril of mist vapour around her finger. She wondered why the mist was so thick all of a sudden, especially when there were no Mist-tribe faeries here to make it. She wasn't going to miss them, she told herself fiercely. The Mists had never wanted her and they'd been glad to see her go.

She hoped the Blaze tribe – and her uncle – would be different.

Laney couldn't settle to anything when she got home. She went over the plan for that evening in her head. Would her uncle's whole family be there? She guessed they would. Her stomach swooped as she pictured it. Maybe her uncle would show her some Blaze spells straightaway.

Finding an excuse for heading out at dusk was tricky too. In Skellmore she'd always been able to say she was going to meet Claudia. She decided to say she was tired and was going to bed early.

In her bedroom, she closed her eyes and waited for that rush of power as her body transformed. Ice-blue wings edged with glowing red unfolded from her back and her skin shimmered. Carefully, she unfastened the window and climbed on to the window sill before launching herself into the darkness. Then she flew straight upwards, feeling the cold air streaming over her skin.

It was so good to fly. She hadn't had the chance lately. There'd been the risk that one of the tribes would notice her altered wings, as well as the danger of being seen by a human. Luckily, their new cottage was outside the village and she could soar right over the fields.

With a sudden burst of energy, she swooped over the cottage roof and glided high into the air. Little stars were speckled across the blackness as if someone had taken a brush coated with glowing white paint and flicked it across the sky. The hills around Little Shackle looked inviting and for a second she wished she could spend all night flying over them. But there was a reason she'd sneaked out. Drifting down, she landed in the lane and switched back to human form. Her coat pocket bulged with her mum's old book, *The Wind in the Willows*. It was the one piece of proof she had that her mum had been Cordelia Embers.

The streets of Little Shackle were empty. Everyone was home for the night, safe behind their drawn curtains. Laney made her way to Tinder Street. Her uncle's house had to be the one where she'd seen Tyler. It was an old cottage with a red front door and creeper climbing over the weather-beaten stones. She raised her hand to use the door knocker and a shock like electricity passed through her.

The red front door...

She remembered it. She'd definitely been here before. Now that she was closer the memories lit up in her mind. She had stood in front of this door and the round brass-coloured door knocker had been far above her head.

"*The last time I saw you was the night Cordelia died*," her uncle had said.

That must be the night she was remembering. Closing her eyes, she tried to think of more – her uncle, her dad, anything ... but she couldn't.

The door swung open. "Are you going to stand out here forever?" Tyler said.

"Hello to you too." Laney tried to smile, but Tyler frowned as he stood aside to let her in.

The inside of the cottage was toasty warm and the flames in the fireplace burned without any coals or wood at all. Connor Embers was sitting in an armchair with his huge legs stretched out. He nodded to Laney as she entered. A woman got up, smiling. She had curly black hair like Tyler's.

"You're right – she's the spit of her father," she said, drawing Laney to the sofa. "Hello. Come and sit down – Elaine, is it?"

"Yes, but everyone calls me Laney," she said, sitting on the sofa.

"I'm Sarah," the woman told her. "It's lovely to

meet you at last."

"I still don't understand why we have to have her here." Tyler's voice had a stubborn note. "The rest of the tribe could find out about her and what she is."

Laney's stomach plummeted. "What do you mean?"

Mr Embers glared at his son. "If you can't open your mouth without being rude then don't speak at all."

"Go and make the tea, please, Tyler," said Mrs Embers hurriedly, and Tyler marched into the kitchen and slammed the door.

"What did he mean?" Laney asked. "Why doesn't he want anyone to know I'm here?"

Her aunt and uncle exchanged looks. Mrs Embers sat beside Laney on the sofa. "I'm sorry he said that. Little Shackle is a very old-fashioned kind of place and it's … unusual for people from different tribes to marry as your parents did. I think Tyler's picked up on things other Blaze kids say. Not that it's any excuse."

"He ought to know better than to copy everyone else," growled her uncle.

"I'll speak to him while you two catch up." Mrs Embers stood up and bustled into the kitchen, leaving Laney alone with her uncle. The fire crackled fiercely in the grate.

"Where's your dad, Laney?" her uncle asked. "Is he all right?"

"He's in hospital in Kirkfield," Laney said, and she told him of the troubles they'd had in Skellmore and how her dad had been struck down by the Shadow.

"A brave man, your father. Always was." Her uncle looked thoughtful. The firelight flickered across his lined face. "And what of the Myricals? We've had patchy reports of events from down south."

Laney explained the finding of the first Myrical last summer. "The Crystal Mirror and the Wildwood Arrow are safe for now," she finished. "They were locked away using the hole in the Mencladden Stone, which stands on a hill outside our village. Gwen, the Thorn Elder, says they're sealed inside Time itself. The spell lasts for a year and a day."

Mr Embers nodded. "We're already looking for our own Myrical, the Sparkstone."

"They're searching for more Myricals around Skellmore too. I was helping before dad got injured—" She broke off, realising that Tyler and his mum had come back in while they'd been talking.

Laney's aunt set a tray with four mugs of tea on the table. "It sounds like it's been terrible in Skellmore," she said quietly. "I'm so sorry to hear about your dad."

"Did that really happen? You saw a Shadow and fought him?" Tyler's eyes narrowed. "You don't look strong enough."

"If someone's blasting you with lightning, you have to defend yourself," said Laney shortly. "I had no choice."

Tyler was silent. Mrs Embers said hurriedly, "So tell us more about where you lived."

Laney described Skellmore and told them how Kim, her stepmum, had brought them to Little Shackle to be near her dad in the hospital.

When she'd finished, her aunt said, "You *have* got a touch of Cordelia about you." She turned to her husband. "See how she tilts her head? That's exactly the way Cordelia used to sit."

Laney reached for her coat and took out *The Wind in the Willows*. "I wanted to show you this." She passed it to Mrs Embers. "It was my mum's and she wrote her name in it." An odd expression passed across her uncle's face but Laney carried on eagerly. "And not very long ago, I found out I could do this." She held out her hand and a flame burst from her palm.

"It's just strange that you don't look like a Blaze," Tyler said.

Laney's heart dropped and the flame in her hand died.

Her uncle rubbed his beard. "If she has Blaze power, she's a Blaze. That's how it works. You can only have one kind of power, even if your parents came from different tribes."

Laney shifted uncomfortably. She hadn't told them the whole story. For a long while after Awakening, she'd used Mist magic even though it hadn't worked very well. It was only months later that her Blaze abilities had appeared. The line from the red moon prophecy popped into her head: *The Child of Aether joins together powers far apart.*

She wasn't some strange Child of Aether though. At least she didn't think so. She didn't actually know what Aether was.

There was a knock at the door and Mrs Embers peeped behind the curtains. "It's Alfred and those Elders from the south." Her eyes flicked to Laney. "Do you think they know she's here?"

"Probably not." Mr Embers got up. "But it'd be best if she wasn't seen until we've decided how to introduce her to the Blaze tribe."

"What's wrong?" Laney asked. "Who's here?"

"Some Elders from the south arrived here this afternoon," her uncle told her. "I think they want to talk about the Shadow and what can be done. Tyler, take Laney into the kitchen and don't come out till I call you."

Tyler grabbed *The Wind in the Willows* and shoved it at Laney. Then he half pushed her into the kitchen and shut the door behind them. The front door banged and there were voices in the living room. With a jolt, Laney realised she was listening to people she knew from Skellmore – Gwen Whitefern and Lucas Frogley, the Mist Elder. Why had they come?

She and Tyler leaned close to the door to listen. She couldn't hear everything. Now and then she caught words like *Shadow* and *Myrical*. It seemed that their visit was all about the threat from the Shadow faerie and plans for finding the three remaining Myricals. Tired, she pulled out a chair, accidentally scraping it along the floor.

"Shh! They'll hear you," Tyler hissed.

There was a lull in the talking next door and they both stopped to listen. The front door banged again.

Laney stared at Tyler's frowning face. He seemed so determined not to like her. "Why are you being like this?"

"Being like what? Am I supposed to be happy I've got a cousin whose dad was a Mist? There's a name they'll call you – the other kids."

Laney's stomach turned over. "What are you talking about?"

Mrs Embers opened the kitchen door. "You can come out now. They've gone. They came to see us because your uncle is a senior member of the Blaze tribe. They've gone to talk some more at Alfred's place. Alfred is the head of our tribe," she added to Laney. Then she noticed the expression on their faces. "What's going on?"

Laney felt as if something was stuck in her throat. "Go on! Tell me," she said to Tyler. "What's the name for someone like me?"

Laney's aunt looked shocked. "Tyler! Your dad and I have taught you better than that. We've said it lots of times – it's unusual to marry someone of a different tribe but we don't use that word."

"I didn't!" said Tyler. "She just asked what the name was—"

"That's enough, Tyler!" Mrs Embers laid a hand on Laney's arm. "Laney, I know it must be strange being here but we're so happy to meet you at last—"

"But you don't want people to know we're related, do you?" Laney interrupted. "That's why you made me go and hide."

"No, that's not true!" said her aunt. "We're happy you found us. We just want to introduce you to the Blaze tribe in the right way."

"You're ashamed of me!" Laney's eyes stung, but there was no way she was going to cry.

"No, not at all!" said Mrs Embers. "It's just difficult. The Blaze Elder doesn't know that you're here yet. We want to speak to him first before everyone meets you."

"Because my parents were from different tribes?" Laney felt heat surge through her fingers. A charred stain spread across *The Wind in the Willows* cover and she quickly shoved the book under her arm. "I have to go – Kim will wonder where I am." She rushed to the front door and ran out into the night.

Once she was out of sight of the cottage, she stopped and wiped her eyes on her jumper sleeve. Even her tears seemed to burn these days.

CHAPTER

6

Bright sunshine blazed down on the hills around Little Shackle the following morning. The empty blue-ness of the sky made Laney sad. There was a hollow in her chest which hadn't been there the day before. She'd been so excited about going to her uncle's house and getting to know her mum's family. But now she wasn't sure they'd been excited to meet her too.

Kim and Toby had gone out. Laney stood at the window staring at the sky for a while. There was only one cloud up there – a thin column right above the pale hill she'd climbed yesterday. It looked strange, as if someone had drawn a white line pointing at the peak.

A magpie flew down to the apple tree in the garden and started pecking off the blossom. Laney banged on the window to scare it away. The rhyme that Kim always said about magpies popped into her head:

One for sorrow
Two for joy
Three for a girl
Four for a boy
Five for silver
Six for gold
Seven for a secret that's never to be told

The magpie flew off in a flash of black-and-white wings.

There was a knock at the door and Laney opened it to find Tyler standing there. She flushed. "What do you want? I don't want to talk to you."

"You left this at our house last night." He handed over Laney's coat.

"Oh! Thanks." Laney started to shut the door but Tyler put his hand on it.

"Want to go for a walk?" He jerked his head at the hills.

"Why? I thought you didn't want a cousin like me – someone with parents from different tribes."

Tyler shifted his feet. "Look, don't make me do the whole apology thing. I was an idiot, OK? The rest of the Blazes can stuff it. We're cousins – family – my blood is your blood."

Laney thought this sounded a bit gross. "Aren't you afraid of what your tribe will say if they see us together?"

"My aunt and uncle have gone to talk to the Blaze Elder so everyone will know about you soon anyway," Tyler said, in a way that Laney didn't find very reassuring. "If you come for a walk I'll show you how to control a flame. You know you're not lighting it properly, right? Don't you want to know how to do it? It's the most basic thing every Blaze kid learns when they first get their powers."

Laney smiled. She realised her anger had vanished as quickly as it had appeared. Maybe a quick temper was a Blaze quality, but Tyler certainly seemed to bring it out in her! She shrugged her coat on. "I definitely want to learn some Blaze spells. I feel like there's lots I don't know."

Tyler turned right and led them away from the village. This was the side of the valley Laney hadn't explored yet – the side with the deep chasm cut into the hillside. Tyler gave her a sideways look. "So what happened when you fought the Shadow? I didn't hear all the things you told my dad last night. Was it scary fighting him? Did you use your lightning?"

"I've never used a lightning spell. You can't use them till you're eighteen."

"Yeah, well. That's supposed to be the rule here too but we use them all the time."

It was Laney's turn to shoot a sideways look. She couldn't believe he'd used lightning spells. He couldn't be any older than her. Maybe he was exaggerating. "I can't remember much about the fight. A lot of it's a blur." Suddenly she remembered the smell of Shadow's cloak burning. She didn't think there was a way to explain what it had been like. Just thinking of it made her feel sick.

Tyler didn't press her. Opening a gate, he took them along a path which led up the hillside. Clumps of heather dotted the grass. "Those Elders of yours have left the village. I saw them go this morning."

Laney was glad they were gone. She didn't want to run into Frogley, the Mist Elder. "They're not *my* Elders."

"You know what I mean. My dad said they mostly talked ancient history – what happened the day the Myricals were lost. Stuff about the Great Shadow of Old."

"I think that's when the Myricals were first hidden." Laney tried to remember the details that she'd learned from Gwen. "They were taken away in secret so that the Great Shadow didn't get hold of them. Each one would have given him the essence of a tribe's power. Once he got them all he'd have become invincible!"

"And now there's a new Shadow that wants to do the same," Tyler said grimly. "Well, he won't get our Blaze Myrical, the Sparkstone. Not unless he wants to fight all of us!"

"What's the Sparkstone like?" Laney asked curiously. "I've seen pictures and it looks quite small and grey."

"I've never seen the Sparkstone because it was lost the same as the other Myricals," Tyler told her. "But my dad's talked about it. He said although it looks like a rough stone you can tell there's a huge amount of power inside – almost like it has a heart made of fire."

They were close to the top now and Little Shackle had shrunk behind them. Huge square boulders were stacked on the hilltop, as if giants had been playing Lego. The wind was blasting from all directions and a bird of prey wheeled overhead. Tyler glanced around before walking down to a hollow just below the brow of the hill. Laney followed him. The wind wasn't so fierce here and little purple flowers grew among the rocks.

"OK, here's the first thing you have to know," he began. "The flame doesn't come from your hand – not really. It comes from inside you." He held up his hand and a flame burst into life, tall and straight and golden.

"What? I don't get it." Laney pushed back her hair as the wind tried to whip it across her face.

"It's not your hand making it happen," he said impatiently. "You have to feel it – in your stomach. Once you understand that, you'll be able to control it a lot better. Now you try."

Laney held her breath. Opening her hand she tried to believe that something inside her would light the flame. "Er, this isn't really working."

"That's because you're so tense. Try to chill!"

He's so annoying, Laney thought crossly, and a flame sprung up in the palm of her hand without her even trying.

Tyler gave a lopsided smile. "Huh – finally! You know, the other tribes say that Blaze magic is the most dangerous faerie power – more random than the magic of the other tribes? But I reckon they're just jealous that we have more heart and soul. Who wants to make things grow or make it rain when you can do this?" And he moved his hand in a circle until he was standing inside a ring of fire. Then he dropped his arm and stood there, grinning, with flames hanging around him in mid-air.

"Show-off!" Laney said, but she couldn't help admiring his skill.

More heart and soul.

Was that how her mum had felt about being a Blaze too? She remembered the first time she had made fire – how good it had felt – like a piece of her had been missing till that moment. As she thought about it she lost concentration for a second and a fireball burst out of her right hand and shot into the air.

"Hey – calm down!" Tyler looked alarmed. "You'll set the hillside on fire."

"Sorry!" Laney closed her hand and the flame went out.

"Bit crazy, aren't you? First you can't make a flame and then you're shooting fireballs everywhere."

Laney rolled her eyes. "So tell me how to control it if you're so clever."

"Just don't let the fire take over." Frowning, Tyler leapt out of the hollow and looked down the hillside before turning back to her. "Don't do anything weird, OK? The others are coming."

"What others?" Laney climbed out of the hollow.

"Other Blaze tribe kids."

Laney's heart quickened. "So what!? You told me you didn't care about what they said."

"I don't!" He was pacing over the hilltop. "But don't do that fireball thing in front of them."

Laney raised her eyebrows.

The kids were calling to him. There were three of them. A girl with red hair and two boys who looked like brothers, both tall and skinny.

"Wotcha doing, Tyler?" said the red-headed girl, with a glance at Laney that made it obvious her question meant: *Who's she?*

"Just hanging out." Tyler dug his hands into his jeans pocket. "This is my cousin Laney. She's from the south."

The older boy stared. "Is she a—"

"Blaze. Yeah, of course." Tyler waved a hand at the girl. "Laney, this is Briana, and this is Zac and Callum."

"Hi." Laney tried to smile but the others were staring and she just felt awkward.

"So what are you guys up to?" said Tyler. "Going over to Beggar's Chasm?"

"Course we are!" Zac grinned at Laney. "You should come with us. Anyone visiting Little Shackle has to do Beggar's Chasm at least once."

Tyler started walking on with Briana and Callum. Laney followed behind with Zac. "So what do you do there?"

"Oh, picnics, ice cream, that kind of thing!"

Laney could tell he was joking. The Blaze kids sped up and the hill narrowed into a ridge of rock with a sheer drop on either side. The others ran along the jagged rocky edge but it took all Laney's concentration to keep her balance and by the time she reached a wider stretch of hillside she felt pretty shaky.

Tyler and the others were laughing and joking together. They'd stopped on a flat expanse of stone that broke off at a cliff edge. Laney realised this must be the deep chasm that she'd seen from the village. As she got closer, she saw just how deep it was. The narrow valley was littered with boulders and a tiny stream ran along the middle. Threads of mist drifted through the air below.

Faint voices came with the mist – a high-pitched singing that made Laney's skin prickle. There must be a faerie ring somewhere down there. She shivered and wrapped her arms around herself. She could never hear those voices without wondering what it was like on the other side. Rings were the doorways to the Otherworld where faerie souls went after death. Immense power surged through the vortex and no one had ever survived falling into one.

Laney suddenly realised Zac was talking to her.

"When you live in a place with nothing to do, you have to make your own entertainment." He grinned as he backed away from the edge. Then he leaned forwards, preparing to run.

It took Laney a few seconds to realise what he was doing. Her heart beat double fast as he sprinted towards the chasm. Launching off the cliff, he sailed through the air – arms wheeling. Then his heels slammed down on the rock on the other side, sending a volley of stones tumbling into the chasm. He got his balance and turned to laugh at the others, the wind ruffling his hair.

Laney's stomach lurched. The chasm was really wide and if he'd fallen, the faerie ring was down there waiting to suck him in.

"OK, my turn." Tyler backed up to give himself room to take a run-up.

"Is this what you do up here?" Laney demanded. "Don't be stupid – you'll kill yourself!"

Tyler spread his arms. "I've done it before and I'm still here, aren't I? The trick is not to think about falling." He raced to the edge and jumped. Sailing over the drop, he flung his arms out and started to come down fast. Laney knew he wasn't going to make it. The world slowed down and in that frozen second, she wondered why she cared so much about Tyler.

Maybe he was right. Her blood was his blood.

She jerked forwards. "Tyler!" But he'd already disappeared into the chasm. Why weren't the others doing something? "You should've stopped him!"

Briana looked at her scornfully. "We didn't need to – look!"

Tyler flew straight past her, transformed with his dark-red wings. "Don't panic, cuz! It's easy." He rocketed across the chasm and landed next to Zac on the other side, still laughing.

Laney glared. He was such an idiot. "Changing in mid-air's really hard to do," she yelled. "If you'd done it any slower you'd have crashed."

"Don't be such a baby," Briana said, and she leapt over the chasm, landing neatly on the other side.

Callum went next. He seemed to find it easy with his long legs. Then Laney was left by herself, staring across the chasm at the others.

"Go on – you can do it," Briana called. "You just have to be ready to switch form in mid-air if you need to."

"Don't bother, Laney. We'll come back over," shouted Tyler and then he said something under his breath to the others. Laney could guess what he was saying. He didn't think she could make it across.

Blood thumped in her ears. Her hands grew hot and she closed them tightly. Without stopping to think, she backed up, ran at the cliff and jumped.

CHAPTER
7

The ground vanished beneath her.

She was used to being in mid-air but not in human form. She felt so heavy with no wings to lift her up.

Falling … falling…

Air rushed past and the singing of the faerie ring reached up to encircle her. Tyler's face above grew smaller and smaller. He was yelling something but she couldn't really hear him.

Wings! she thought. *I need my wings.*

Switching just in time, her wings opened wide and caught the wind. She hovered shakily and when she landed on the grass at the bottom her panic faded. It was really beautiful down here. Rocky cliffs rose on both sides and a stream poured along the valley bottom. At one end, a dark cave opened into the cliffs, its mouth strewn with boulders. The faerie ring was further along the chasm. She could hear the ghostly singing near a waterfall that cascaded down the cliff face.

In a swirl of wings, Tyler and the others landed beside her. "You should've just waited for us," Tyler snapped, switching to human form.

Laney changed back too and folded her arms. "What's the problem? You brought me here and you jumped first. I just did the same as you."

"Yeah, Tyler." Briana looked amused. "She might

be a southern girl but she can still fly."

Tyler grunted and went to join Zac and Callum, who were climbing over the boulders beside the cliff.

"Boys, huh?" Briana snapped her fingers to conjure a flame and aimed it at a nearby boulder, making a pattern in soot before scuffing it off with her shoe. "So ... your wings are cool. I've never seen any with two colours before." She eyed Laney curiously. "It's weird that you haven't come to visit before, seeing as you're Tyler's cousin. Are your mum and dad here too?"

"I..." Laney hadn't really thought about what she was going to tell everyone. Best to stick to the truth – as much of it as she could tell right now. "My dad's ill in hospital and my stepmum's renting a place on the edge of the village."

Briana's eyebrows rose and Laney dreaded what she'd want to know next, but she seemed to get distracted. "I don't believe it. Is he spying on us now?" She called to the others. "Hey, we've got company!"

Zac jerked round and his face tightened.

"What is it?" Laney looked past Briana and saw a man further down the valley wearing a green anorak with the hood pulled right up.

"Hey, you!" Callum yelled, but the man didn't turn round.

"Who's that?" asked Laney. "Is he from the Blaze tribe?"

"No." Briana's eyes were cold. "That's Christopher Delaney. He runs a chip shop in town so we call him Chips Delaney and basically he's a Tainted."

"What?" Laney had a terrible sickening sensation – as if she could see a punch coming straight at her. What was a Tainted?

"This is a Blaze place and he shouldn't be here," Callum told her.

"He's a Tainted," Briana repeated. "One of his parents was a Thorn and the other was a Blaze so, when you think about it, that makes him nothing at all."

"One of us should go and tell him to stay away." Zac shot a fireball at the ground and a patch of grass curled up and turned black.

"Just leave it, Zac. He's not worth it." Tyler looked at Laney. The message in his eyes was – *don't say anything*.

"A Tainted?" Laney knew her voice sounded funny. "So that's what you call it." This was what Tyler had been talking about last night. It was the name for mixed-tribe people. Tainted.

"He hates us," Zac told her. "One time he came to Groaning Tor on the night of the Kindling and tried to wreck the Bale Fire." He misread the look on Laney's face. "You know – the Bale Fire. Don't you have that in the south?"

"Come on, let's go." Briana started walking along the ravine. "This is just getting boring."

Laney stared at the figure in the green anorak. Just as he got to a bend in the path he glanced back before disappearing behind the fold of the hillside.

Tyler waited for Laney, hanging back behind the others. "Are you OK? I know it must be weird but—"

"So that's what I am, then? A *Tainted*," Laney hissed. "You know I'm exactly the same as that man, and your friends will know soon too. All that rubbish about how I seem different because I'm from the south... I might as well just tell them."

"Leave it for now," Tyler told her. "My parents will sort things out with our Elder. Anyway you're not like Chips Delaney."

"I can't believe he's that bad."

"He hates us. He lives in the huge house with big gates just down the road from the garage and he sets his dog on us if we go anywhere near the place." Tyler marched off, leaving Laney seething. She couldn't believe he wanted her to hide who she was. He was ashamed of her again and the way Briana had talked about that man made her stomach heave.

The Blaze kids took the path alongside the stream and Laney followed them reluctantly. She passed the waterfall that cascaded down the cliff face. The spray drifted through the air, glittering in rainbow colours. Just beyond that was a ring of dark grass and Laney's skin began to prickle as she drew closer. The song of the faerie ring was high and sweet and the air around it was brimming with magic.

Laney sped up. Her shoulders tightened and she tried not to think about the things that Briana and the others had said. The singing inside the ring grew so loud it made her head whirl. Eyes stinging, she stumbled over a rock on the edge of the stream and fell on to her hands and knees.

One voice inside the ring sang out, lifting above the noise of the others. She thought she knew that voice – that song – but where did she know it from?

She stumbled to her feet, leaning closer to the ring. "Hello? It's me, Laney."

The voice faltered. Then it echoed her name.

Laney's heart raced. Faeries passed to the Otherworld when they died. Maybe the voice belonged to her mum? She took a deep breath. "Mum, is that you?" There was no reply so she tried again. "Cordelia Embers?"

The voice sang again. Laney felt it was trying to tell her something. She leaned even closer, catching the words, *"water"*, *"fire"* and *"love"*. A handful of water drops lifted from the surface of the stream nearby and hung glittering in the air. An air current caught them, sending them swirling in circles before they vanished into the ring.

The voice that Laney recognised finished her song. Laney held her breath. Had she just used Mist magic to move those water drops? It had been so long since she'd managed to make a Mist spell work. She glanced along the rocky valley. She didn't want the other Blaze kids to spot her using water magic, but they were too far away to have seen anything.

"Goodbye," Laney whispered to the ring. She promised herself that she'd return as soon as she could.

When Laney got back to Pebblenook Cottage, Claudia's mum's car was parked outside.

Claudia opened the cottage door. "I was starting to think I'd have to come and find you."

"It's so great to see you!" Laney hugged her.

Claudia grinned. "Are you missing Skellmore? I persuaded my mum that we should come and visit. She and Kim are in the back garden. Come and tell me what's been going on."

Laney took off her coat and followed Claudia inside. "Is that the whole reason you're here?" She checked Toby and Kim weren't within earshot before adding, "Or is it partly because of the Myricals and the Shadow?"

"Sort of. Some of our Elders came to talk to the northern tribes."

"I bet the Blazes said they didn't want any help finding the Sparkstone."

Claudia nodded. "That's what my mum told me. I think they were pretty fierce about it. Anyway, my mum's thinking of sending me to stay at my aunt's house in Kirkfield for a while. She thinks the Skellmore tribes will go to war against each other. There's already a curfew and no one except the Elders are allowed out after dark."

"Really? That's great!" Laney's eyes lit up. "Obviously not about the tribes, but I'd love you to stay in Kirkfield. When will your mum decide?"

"In the next couple of weeks," Claudia told her. "Then if I come here I'd start at the school in Kirkfield after half-term. So do you like it here so far?"

"I found out that my uncle and his family live here," Laney said. "But I'm not sure I like the other Blaze kids." Laney told Claudia about what had happened with Tyler at Beggar's Chasm and the man in the green anorak.

"Seriously, chasm jumping?" Claudia raised her eyebrows. "I've heard that the Blaze faeries can be daredevils, but you're not like that."

Secretly, Laney was worried that was exactly her problem – she wasn't like the Blaze kids at all.

She hadn't told Claudia what had happened at the faerie ring with the water drops. It was too weird to even try to explain. She shifted the conversation back to the man in the green anorak. "They said he had parents from different tribes and they called him a Tainted." She felt her palms growing hotter.

"I've heard that name before and it really sucks." Claudia looked sympathetic. "But I guess a lot of faeries think that way. Hardly anyone marries outside their tribe."

"Some people do! My mum and dad did."

"Have you told them that yet? You should, you know."

Laney folded her arms. "I know! It's just—"

"Claudia, time to go." Mrs Lionhart called from the garden.

Laney said goodbye. Going up to her room, she watched from her window as Claudia and her mum drove away. She hoped Mrs Lionhart would decide that Claudia should stay with her aunt in Kirkfield. It wouldn't be so lonely with Claudia around.

On the roof above, she heard the chattering cry of a magpie. She pulled the curtains closed and sat on her bed. Turning her palm upwards, she lit a flame by feeling the fire inside her just as Tyler had said. The flame burned steadily – a blaze of orange with a bright golden centre. She wouldn't let anyone say she wasn't a proper Blaze, she told herself fiercely. She had fire magic and she was determined to get better at using it.

CHAPTER

8

Laney started her new school on Monday. It was in the town of Kirkfield not far from the hospital, and was smaller than the one she had gone to in Skellmore. On the first day she passed Briana and the other Blaze kids going into the cafeteria but they didn't speak to her. She guessed they'd heard by now that she had parents from different tribes and that was why they were keeping away. After their argument, Tyler didn't seek her out either. She longed for Claudia to move to her aunt's but there was no message from her friend and she started to wonder if Claudia's mum had changed her mind.

Every Friday, Laney visited the hospital after school. After three weeks the school broke up for half-term. As she hurried down the hospital corridor that afternoon she wondered if she'd hear any news from Claudia soon. She had no idea what was going on in Skellmore these days or how Fletcher and the other Thorns were.

Sitting down by her dad's bed, she listened to the beep of the heart-rate monitor and watched the numbers on the machine going up and down. Careful not to knock the drip, she held her dad's hand and searched his face for a sign that he knew she was there. She told him about their cottage in Little Shackle and the circle of hills around the village. She talked about Kim and Toby, and how

Simon was looking after their business back in Skellmore.

She even told him how she'd been back to Beggar's Chasm a second time to speak to the voice she recognised inside the faerie ring. This time, the voice had seemed clearer and she had realised it was a young voice, so maybe it didn't belong to her mum after all. It was difficult to pick out the words with so many other voices singing.

Running out of things to say to her dad, she clasped his hand tighter. At first he'd seemed better in this new place but now his skin was so pale and crumpled. Her eyes filled with tears and she gathered up her school bag. She wanted to hope but each time she came here she felt like her heart was being squeezed. She hurried out into the cold evening air and caught the bus back to Little Shackle.

Walking up the lane from the bus stop, she saw someone leaning against the garden wall. Darkness was gathering and the figure was holding a small flame which flickered red then white then gold.

It had to be Tyler.

As she got closer he lifted the flame, turning his skin gold and his eyes glittering black. "Hey! I'm starting to think you're avoiding me."

"No, you're avoiding me." Laney walked past him to the gate.

"We just had an argument – no big deal," he said, grinning. "What happened to being cousins? Don't you like me any more?"

Laney wasn't in the mood for this. "Did your parents make you come here? Look, I'm fine by myself. You know you don't really want to hang out with me and you can't use Blaze power outside our house. Our neighbour might see."

Tyler's flame vanished into smoke. "I do want to hang out with you."

"I don't believe you." Laney banged the gate behind her. "You didn't want your friends to find out what I am and that proves you're bothered."

"So now you're telling me I'm a liar. Thanks a lot."

"What did you expect?" Laney snapped. A flame burst to life in her hand and she let go of the gate quickly so she didn't burn it. "I saw the way you all treated that 'Chips' guy."

"Leave him out of it," Tyler snapped. "Believe it or not I actually came to say I'd teach you Blaze skills. The Kindling's on May the first and that's only a few weeks away. It's a big thing for us Blazes. We go up into the hills and light the Bale Fire. If you want to join in you need to learn to control your power and you need to know what to do. So it's up to you: do you want to be a proper Blaze or not?" He clicked his fingers, showering the path with sparks, and walked off without waiting for an answer.

Laney went in, slamming the front door behind her. Why did Tyler always make her so cross? It felt strange to have this hot temper bubbling inside her. What made it even stranger was that she knew she actually really liked Tyler – when he wasn't being annoying. She sighed. She should've accepted his offer of help. Now she'd have to go and apologise. She suddenly realised that the cottage was dark and silent.

"Kim, are you here?" She switched the light on and went into the kitchen. There was a note lying on the table.

Hi Laney, Simon drove up from Skellmore to see us and he's going to take us to the hospital to see your dad. We'll be back later and I'll bring a takeaway for dinner. See you soon, love Kim.

Laney put down the note. Making a quick decision, she dumped her school bag and headed back down the road to the village. The last patches of daylight were fading behind the hills. She could just about make out Groaning Tor, the tallest peak. Flickers of orange burst from the summit, making her catch her breath. It had to be Blaze magic, only visible to faerie eyes. Tyler had told her the peak was important to the Blaze tribe, she remembered.

There was a light on inside the bakery and Laney breathed in the warm smell of baking bread. She carried on walking till she reached her uncle's repair shop. Stopping outside, she stared at the *Embers* name written on the window. She should go over to her uncle's house and apologise to Tyler. Then she should tell him how much she wanted to learn more Blaze skills.

She frowned. It was true – she did want to learn fire spells – but she felt like something else was drawing her on. What was it? She walked on, trying to make sense of the spinning thoughts inside her head. Why had she come all the way here in the dark? What was she looking for?

Halfway along the street she came to a stop. She was standing outside the house with the high walls and the big iron gate that she'd noticed before. From what Tyler had said, she was pretty sure that Chips Delaney lived here. He was the man whose parents had come from different tribes. The man they called a Tainted.

That was why she was here. She wanted to see him.

She tried to open the gate but it was padlocked. A blinding light flicked on overhead and a dog started barking.

"Mr Delaney?" Laney called out. "Sorry to bother you. Can I talk to you, just for a minute?"

The barking got louder and a great black dog bounded down the drive and threw itself at the gate, snarling and snapping. Laney fell back. This was stupid. Why would he agree to talk to her anyway?

"Get away from my gate or I'll set Gutter on you!" A dark figure with a torch rounded the corner of the drive and came right up to the gate.

Laney couldn't see past the glare of the overhead light but she knew it must be Chips Delaney. "I'm sorry, I just—"

"You can shout abuse and throw rotten stuff over my walls," he growled. "But if you set one foot on my property my dog will tear you to shreds."

Seeing the dog's jagged white teeth, Laney could totally believe it. "I haven't come to throw stuff. I just wanted to ask you something." She knew it sounded lame.

"Ha, that's a good one!" A torch beam fixed on her – blinding her even more. "You're the girl I saw at Beggar's Chasm with those Blaze kids. So why would I believe a word you say?"

Laney backed away. "Fine, I'll go. I only came because I'm like you – my parents were from different tribes – and I wanted to talk to you about it."

"Wait!" There was a clanking as a key turned in the padlock and Chips Delaney opened the gate. Laney tensed, waiting for the animal to spring at her but on a gruff word from its owner, the dog sat down and wagged its tail. Mr Delaney towered over

Laney, his thin face caught in the security light. "You're not from around here, are you? Who are you? Why are you running with the Blaze crowd if you're not like them?"

Laney swallowed. "I have Blaze powers because my mum was a Blaze. But my dad's a Mist." Mr Delaney didn't answer and Laney hurried to fill the silence. "I'm Laney Rivers."

"What do you mean your mum *was* a Blaze?" interrupted Delaney. "What happened to her?"

"She got ill and died when I was little. Her name was Cordelia Embers."

Delaney swore under his breath. He hesitated before opening the gate wider. "You'd better come in." He closed the gate and fastened the padlock behind her. The security light pinged off as they walked up the drive. In the faint light over the front door, Laney could see a run-down garden, covered with brambles and broken pots. The house was huge and square and had shutters over the windows.

Mr Delaney bounded up the steps to the door and glanced back as Laney hesitated. "You're quite safe, I promise you," he said. "Just ask Gutter."

Laney jumped as the shaggy black dog licked her hand before trotting into the house. The change from terrifying guard dog to soppy pet was strange but reassuring and Laney followed them in, shutting the door behind her. The house and the things in it looked like something out of a museum – tarnished brass candlesticks and black-and-white photos. There was even a wooden spinning wheel in the corner. A brown-leaved cactus stood on the mantelpiece.

Delaney had collapsed in a tattered armchair with Gutter lying across his feet, tail thumping. He leaned down to pat the dog and then stared into the empty fireplace. Laney realised he wasn't as old as she'd first thought but his deep eyes and thin face made him look sad. "So you're Cordelia's daughter," he said. "I didn't know she'd married a Mist – not that I ever get told the news around here. That must have been an upset at the time."

Laney twisted her jumper sleeve. "Did you know my mum?"

"Only a little. She was a few years older than me. There is something of you about her." He shot her a curious look. "A Blaze marrying a Mist, that's something that doesn't happen every day. Which power do you have – water?"

"No, fire." Laney opened her hand and focused on lighting a flame the way Tyler had taught her. It worked beautifully. A dark look flickered across Delaney's eyes – a hunger mixed with despair. It shocked Laney and she quickly closed her hand to put the flame out.

"So what did the brave and noble Blazes tell

you about me?" Delaney asked shortly. "That I'm abnormal – a freak and a Tainted?"

"They said one of your parents was a Blaze and the other a Thorn."

"Yeah, I bet that's not all they said about me." He gave a bitter laugh.

Laney shifted awkwardly on the armchair. This man wasn't exactly easy to talk to, but she needed to find out what was going on with her powers and he was the only one who might know.

She took a deep breath. A question had lurked at the back of her mind like a rat in the dark ever since Beggar's Chasm. "Has your magic ever got mixed up? I'm a Blaze but this one time I used water magic without even meaning to and I wondered if you'd ever had that happen too."

Delaney sprang up, jerking the dog off his feet. "I have NO power! Didn't they tell you that, girl?"

"I'm sorry! I just thought…"

"You thought I'd be a Blaze or a Thorn and I should be! But they took my power away. Hasn't your Mist father told you the stories? Don't you know what they did to the mixed-tribe children?"

Laney met his gaze. "My dad's unconscious in hospital. He's been like that ever since he tried to protect me from the Shadow faerie."

The fierce look faded from Delaney's face and he sat down again. "You're from the south then? I heard there was trouble there. I'm sorry. We should start again." He looked at her for a minute. "I'll make us some tea." He went next door and came back with two steaming mugs of tea. Then he knelt down by the fireplace and struggled with some matches and sheets of newspaper. Finally he got the fire burning. Then he took a large swig of tea and Gutter settled down on his feet again.

"About your magic," he said at last. "If your parents come from different tribes then you only take after one of them. You can't have both powers – it's impossible. When I was young there were a few mixed-tribe children living in Little Shackle and as they grew up each developed the same power as one parent. That's the way it goes. Nature picks for us, I suppose. You must have been mistaken about what you managed to do."

Laney stared into her mug of tea. Her uncle had said the same thing – that faeries only had one kind of power even if their parents came from different tribes. But how had she worked magic on the water that day at Beggar's Chasm? It made no sense. "Where are those other mixed-tribe faeries now?" she asked. "Do they still live nearby?"

Delaney's shoulders stiffened. "Most of them left when it began. I don't know where they went or how long they stayed in hiding." He struggled for words. "A Shadow rose here in the north and no one had the strength to go against him. The Elders believed he came from mixed-tribe parents – I don't know why. So they put their plan into action. Everyone that was mixed tribe was rounded up – all of us who had Awakened, that is."

"So you'd Awakened by then?"

"Yes. One Sunday night when I was eight, I produced a flame – a tiny one. My father was so proud. I think he really wanted me to be a Blaze like him. But by the next morning they were knocking on the door. They must have been watching the house." His jaw clenched. "They called it The Purge. They suspended me from a tree above a fairy ring until all magic power was sucked out of me. Then they cut me down and left me. It was terrifying … and very painful."

Laney looked away. Her hands shook and a little tea slopped over the edge of her mug.

"My parents told me it didn't matter about losing my magic – that I was safe. But I didn't feel safe and I never have since that day." He gave a bitter smile. "I hoped for a while that my Blaze power would return or that in its absence, I would find a little of my mother's Thorn magic, but it wasn't to be. I still keep the same herbs that she did but they don't always grow very well." He glanced at the brown cactus. "I'm afraid plants don't like me any more than people do."

Laney felt sorry for him. How could the other faeries have done something so awful to a child? "But why is everyone here so mean to you?"

Delaney's shoulders sagged. "For a long time, I was very angry and I did some bad things – things I'm not proud of." His face darkened. "They goaded me and when I lashed out, an innocent Blaze girl got hurt. I've never been able to make it right since then," he continued. "The older Blazes don't like me because they remember what happened. The kids just follow what their parents say and so it goes on. I have high walls and a locked gate but that's little defence from people that can fly." He frowned at the fire. "Sometimes they all leave me alone for a while but it always starts up again."

"I'm sure my uncle and aunt don't believe you should be treated badly. They told my cousin off for being mean about mixed-tribe people."

"You mean Connor and Sarah Embers? They've always been polite to me. But don't look for kindness from the others."

Laney bit her lip. "But maybe if we explain … if we make everyone see that we're not so strange, then they'll start to understand."

There were shouts from outside followed by a heavy thunk against the shuttered window. Delaney muttered something under his breath before going to the window and unbolting the shutters.

"Come over here. I'll show you how much they'll understand."

A round missile flew inside and rolled across the floor. In the darkness, winged figures swooped over Delaney's garden.

"Its cabbages this time," said Delaney grimly. "They're probably selling them off cheap at the grocers. You'll never make them understand – they don't *want* to understand. The only reason I stay is because my parents are buried in the churchyard and I've never lived anywhere else. Little Shackle is my home."

Laney swallowed. Her hands burned but she clenched them tight. "I should go. My stepmum will probably be back from the hospital by now."

"It was nice to meet you, Laney." Delaney reached out to close the shutter but a missile shot through the open window, hitting him in the chest. The cabbage fell to the ground and a girl flew past the window, the light catching on her red hair.

"Tainted!" shouted Briana, but the rest of her words died when she saw Laney.

Then Delaney slammed the shutter closed and bolted it.

CHAPTER
9

By the time Laney got outside the sky was empty. Her blood pounded as she flew over the high wall, landed in the street and switched back to human form. There was no sign of Briana but Laney knew she would be telling everyone what she'd seen. It wouldn't take long before everyone knew that she had been here talking to a man that many of the Blazes hated. They'd probably be furious.

She had to get to her uncle's house. He would know what to do.

She ran past Embers' Repairs and round the corner. There was a whisper in the air as she sprinted up her uncle's front path. She stumbled and fell, and her knee smacked into the concrete. It should have been agony but she hardly felt it. Kneeling on the path, she was looking up at the red front door again with memories flooding through her.

She'd been looking at the round door knocker high above her head. Tendrils of creeper had dangled over the stone wall. Her father had been by her side and he'd been holding something – a small brown thing that looked like a purse. He'd given the little purse to her uncle.

Laney's pulse fluttered like a trapped bird. Her uncle had told her he'd last seen her on the night her mum died. Why had they travelled all the way to Little Shackle at a time like that?

The door wrenched open and her aunt pulled

her up. "Laney, thank the flame you've come." She ushered Laney inside and closed the door.

A fire was burning in the living-room grate. Mr Embers and Tyler got up as Laney came in.

Laney spoke quickly. "I went to Chips Delaney's house and Briana saw me there. I'm really sorry. I know most of the Blaze tribe don't like him."

"You went to Chips' house?!" Tyler exploded. "You idiot!"

"Enough, Tyler!" Mrs Embers took Laney's arm. "We were trying to give you time – with your dad in hospital and everything. I wish we'd sorted this out days ago."

"There's no point in wishing." Mr Embers rubbed his beard. "Laney, we've had a message from the Blaze Elder. You've been summoned to see him – right now."

The fire in the grate leapt upwards and Laney's heart thumped faster. Would the Blaze Elder be angry with her? "All right. Just tell me where I need to go."

Mr Embers picked up his coat. "We're coming with you."

Rain was falling and the Embers pulled their hoods up. Laney noticed there were more people than usual out walking in the darkness. They were in small groups and had their heads down. The shops on the main street were dark except for the bakery, where warm orange light seeped out from the edges of the blind.

Mr Embers knocked on the door. The place was crowded with people and Laney guessed they must all be Blazes. They had a similar look – sharp eyes and quick movements. Laney flushed as she followed her uncle, knowing they must be looking at her. They passed the shop counter and entered a second room where heat wrapped around them like a blanket. Everyone shifted backwards, leaving Laney standing alone in the centre. At last she could see the source of the heat – an enormous baker's oven with fire crackling inside it.

A grey-haired bear of a man stood by the oven, resting his hand on the arch of red bricks at the top. "Come here, Elaine Rivers. Let me see you," he said in a gravelly voice.

"That's our Elder, Alfred Hillburn," her aunt whispered to Laney.

The Blaze Elder held out a wrinkled hand for her to shake and studied her with sharp eyes. "Welcome, daughter of Cordelia Embers."

Laney smiled, trying not to show her nerves.

"What power do you have, child?" the Elder asked.

Laney cleared her throat. "Um, Blaze."

"Then light a flame."

Laney carefully produced a flame in one hand. It

was hard to keep it burning steadily with everyone watching, but she managed to keep it tall and straight for a few seconds before letting it go out.

A whisper ran around the place. The room grew hotter until Laney felt as if her hair was scorching and the air burned her throat as she breathed. Just as she felt she couldn't bear it any more, Alfred Hillburn began to speak. "Many years ago, our Blaze daughter, Cordelia Embers, married a man from the Mist tribe. Unhappily she did not live to see her own daughter grow. Cordelia left this place in a time of fear and never returned. This girl possesses our fire magic and her uncle and aunt have claimed her as family."

Laney glanced at her uncle, who stood nodding, his arms folded. Her eyes filled with tears. She was so happy that he and her aunt were standing beside her and showing she was part of their family.

"Laney Rivers," continued Hillburn. "Do you wish to join the Blaze tribe?"

Laney's heart jumped. "Yes, I do."

"But, sir!" called a voice from the back. "Just look at her – she's no Blaze." Other people murmured in agreement.

"That's enough!" The Elder lifted his hand and little snakes of fire writhed around his fingers. "We will give her this chance. If she can pass the first-level tests on the night of the Kindling along with the other young Learners, then she may enter the tribe."

"Thank you, Alfred," said Laney's aunt.

The Blaze Elder nodded. "Now, listen closely. You've all heard the rumours. There's been trouble in the south and a new Shadow has arisen. So this is no time for us to quarrel among ourselves. We must unite and stand together. That's how we stay strong as Blazes." He put his palms together and a spark leapt from them. Every other Blaze did the same. The sparks flew up and joined together like bees in a swarm until they exploded into one ball of flame that leapt into the huge oven and disappeared up the chimney. Laney heard something in the flames. There was a deep thrumming as if the fire had a heartbeat.

There was silence after the fire vanished. Then gradually the Blazes left the bakery. Some of them smiled at Laney and her mood lifted. Not even Briana's scowling face at the back of the room could change the fact that the Elder had said she could join the tribe. Maybe Chips Delaney was wrong about the Blazes.

"Ignore Briana," Tyler said into her ear. "Once you pass the test at the Kindling they'll forget they ever had doubts about you. You'd better let me help with your training though. Your skills are rubbish."

Laney grinned. "OK, that'd be great. When do we start?"

Tyler smiled back. "Tomorrow. Trust me – you have loads to learn."

"All right, you're on." Laney went to Alfred Hillburn, who was talking to her uncle. The room was nearly empty now and the heat from the oven had faded. "Thank you for giving me the chance to become a proper Blaze, sir." She hesitated. "I talked to Chips Delaney, I mean, Mr Delaney, because he's like me and I just wondered—"

Alfred Hillburn held up a wrinkled hand to stop her speaking. "Christopher chose his path many years ago when he attacked other members of his own tribe." He studied her from beneath lowered eyebrows. "I'm not saying that what was done to him was right – I wasn't the Elder then and the methods used were exceptionally cruel. But he can never come back from what he did. Our tribe may be quick to act but we also never forget."

"Oh." Laney bit her lip She remembered the look of hunger in Delaney's eyes when he'd seen her flame. How could people stay angry about things that had happened so long ago?

Her aunt drew her to the door. "Thank goodness that went well," she whispered. "And now you're properly part of this family and everyone knows it."

Laney's eyes stung again. "Thank you."

"You don't need to thank us," her uncle said gruffly. "When your father flew back with you that night and told me what had happened to Cordelia, I thought I'd lost her completely. But now I see I was wrong."

Laney bit her lip. This was more than she'd hoped for – the chance to be a real Blaze like her mum.

Every day of half-term, Laney and Tyler climbed the hills to practise Blaze skills where no one could see them except sheep. Among the rough boulders, Laney learned to control her powers until she could light a flame and put it out again without even thinking about it.

On the Saturday before they went back to school, Tyler was sprawled over a rock near the top of Groaning Tor watching Laney light flames in both hands at once. It was early and the sun had barely risen over Beggar's Chasm on the opposite side of the valley. Laney was in a cheerful mood. Simon had stayed the night at the cottage and slept on the sofa. Kim was happy after the doctors had told her that Mr Rivers was making "good progress" – whatever that meant.

Laney had told Kim that she was meeting up with a friend that morning. She knew she'd have to introduce Tyler to her stepmum soon and explain that she'd found her uncle, aunt and cousin living here in Little Shackle. She just needed to find the right moment to do it.

"She can't have been a very normal kind of Blaze," Tyler said suddenly.

"What do you mean – who can't have been a normal Blaze?" Laney shooed a magpie off a nearby boulder. The bird flew to the next patch of rocks and perched there, its head tilted to one side. Laney noticed how still the bird was. She felt like it was watching her with those beady black eyes.

"Hey, stop daydreaming!" Tyler said, grinning. "I was talking about your mum. A Blaze marrying a Mist is pretty strange. It's not like fire and water really go together."

Laney didn't answer this but privately she'd been wondering about her mum too. All she remembered was her mother's dark eyes, short brown hair and kind smile. Sometimes she didn't know if she recalled those things because she'd looked at her mum's photo so many times. Maybe it wasn't a real memory at all.

Before going to sleep the night before, she'd got out *The Wind in the Willows*, the book that had belonged to her mum. She'd leafed through the pages of the story looking at the finely drawn pictures of Toad, Ratty and Mole in a boat on the river. The river seemed to be in a lot of the drawings. She guessed most Blaze children wouldn't love endless pictures of water. Where had her mum even got the book from?

"Shall I teach you something new?" Tyler got up. "Let's try the other side of the hill. The wind's picking up and we need a bit more shelter."

Laney followed him to the top of Groaning Tor where the wind battered them even harder. Jutting rocks cast sharp shadows across the hillside and Little Shackle looked like a tiny model village below.

As they clambered over the summit, Laney glanced at the crevice in the white rock. "Why is this place called Groaning Tor? I've wanted to ask someone for ages." She leaned closer to the hole and felt heat on her face.

"Sometimes the hill sort of rumbles," Tyler told her. "The story goes that there's a fire giant hidden under the ground and he's making the groaning noises."

Laney remembered the sparks she'd seen coming out of the peak a week ago. "It's not true, is it?"

Tyler rolled his eyes. "Well, duh! Of course it's not! Now, can we make a start?" He sprang down to a flat expanse of rock below the peak. "Come over here. If you drop your fireballs on rock there won't be patches of burned grass everywhere."

"Fireballs! I definitely want to learn how to do that." Laney's eyes gleamed.

Tyler showed her how to take a flame and mould

it into a ball before throwing it across the hillside. It took a lot of practice because when pressed too hard the flame would go out but when moulded too lightly the ball would fizzle away in mid-air. After a while Laney began to get the hang of it. She made a perfect golden fireball and the wind whipped it sideways straight into Tyler.

"Whoa, steady!" Tyler laughed, batting it away with one hand. "I guess now you can make them we'd better practise throwing them." He made a fireball of his own and threw it at her like it was a tennis ball.

She caught it and squeezed it hard to put it out. It still amazed her that the fire never hurt. "So what else do I need to know for the Kindling?"

"You still need to learn frost flames and circles of fire and how to melt stuff." He ticked each thing off on his hand. "I forget what else. I'll ask my dad. We've got till the first of May so no need to panic."

"I've never heard of frost flames. How do you make them?"

"Let's do that next time. There's no point doing too much work." Tyler moulded three fireballs and started trying to juggle with them. He dropped one on his trainer and had to stamp it out quickly. It left a black scorch mark on the toe.

Laney watched, a little annoyed that he'd stopped teaching her. "I thought my skills were rubbish and

I had loads of work to do."

"We can do more next time."

Laney gave up. Obviously Tyler had the attention span of a small fly. He made another fireball and spun it on the top of his finger. Laney noticed something on the inside of his wrist. "You've got a burn mark like mine." She showed him the red circle on her middle finger that still prickled sometimes. "I got mine the first time I touched a flame. Nothing's ever burned me since then."

"It's your dawn mark, right? You got it when you Awakened?" He saw Laney's puzzled look. "All Blazes have them. We Awaken as Blazes when our power is ready but we have to touch fire to start it all off. I guess that's not such a big thing for a Mist or a Greytail – people are touching water and animals all the time. But a Blaze must touch fire because that's our thing." His brow creased. "I guess you haven't had anyone to tell you this stuff."

"Um, not really." Laney's brain was working furiously. Suddenly all her dad's efforts to keep matches and candles out of the house made more sense. He must have been afraid she'd Awaken as a Blaze.

"Uh-oh." Tyler stopped twirling his fireball.

Briana was climbing the hillside, her red hair swirling in the wind.

"What's she doing here?" Laney stuck her hands

in her pockets. There was no way she was practising Blaze magic in front of Briana.

"Tyler!" Briana called. "You've got to come back – quickly!"

"What's going on?" Tyler sprang over the rocks to meet her.

"There was a Shadow faerie," Briana said breathlessly. "He was at Cowton Lane near the crossroads. Your mum's car was there and she was hurt so they carried her to the cave in Beggar's Chasm. She's there now. They think she's been struck by Shadow lightning."

CHAPTER 10

Tyler's eyes turned wild. "No! The Shadow's down south – not here! It can't be here."

Briana grabbed his arm. "Don't lose it, OK!" And ignoring Laney, she pulled him down the hill.

Laney felt sick. So the Shadow was back and her aunt was hurt. It was the same thing that had happened to her dad all over again. Forcing her legs to move, she ran down the slope after Tyler. By the time she reached the first house in the village, he and Briana were already out of sight. She took the road past her cottage to get to Beggar's Chasm.

As she ran, a familiar blue van came down the street. Simon stopped and lowered the window. "Bye, Laney. I'm going back to Skellmore – I've got another broken pipe to fix this afternoon. No rest for the—" He broke off, frowning. "Has something happened? Look at your hands!"

Laney glanced down. Her palms were glowing red hot. There was no way to hide it. "It's a long story ... but I'm not a Mist any more – I never was, really. Please don't tell anyone from back home."

Simon's eyes went round. "Flippin' heck, Laney! I guess it makes sense because of all the problems you had using Mist magic. Are you all right?"

"I'm fine. But listen! The Shadow's here and he's hurt someone. You have to tell Gwen and ask her to come and help us. We need someone powerful enough to stand up to the Shadow."

Simon's eyebrows rose further and his foot slipped on the pedals, making the car jerk forwards. He pulled the handbrake and wiped his forehead. "That's very bad news. Yes I'll go and speak to her as soon as I get back. Some of the Elders might be travelling here already. I heard that they wanted to discuss searching for the Myricals with the other tribes."

"OK. I have to go!" Laney ran on.

"Be careful," Simon called after her.

The road curved round and a signpost pointed the way to Cowton Lane. A group of Blazes, including Hillburn, the Elder, were gathered at the crossroads. Laney's heart tightened as she saw the wreckage of a car. Its windscreen was shattered – and a long scorch mark zigzagged across the roof. The car lay with its rear end sticking up and its front wheels in a ditch.

Desperate to see her aunt, Laney raced across the field and into the ravine. The cave was right at the opening of the chasm, its entrance lined with jagged rocks like a monster's teeth. Laney clambered along the narrow tunnel, water dripping down her neck from the cave roof. Mrs Embers lay on the rocky ground with Laney's uncle kneeling beside her and Tyler pacing up and down. Briana leaned against the cave wall nearby and she swung round to glare at Laney.

"How is she?" Laney's voice echoed off the walls.

Tyler didn't seem to hear the question. He stopped pacing and fire blazed in his hands. "We have to go after this Shadow. Right now."

"You can't!" Laney burst out. "He's so powerful! Hardly anyone is strong enough to face him."

Tyler clenched his fists. "I can't just do nothing!"

Laney touched his arm. "Don't go after him, please! I've already seen my dad get hurt..."

Mr Embers leaned over his wife. "Sarah, can you hear me?"

Mrs Embers didn't move.

Laney's throat tightened. Her aunt was so pale and still. Why had the Shadow come here? And why now? Was he searching for another Myrical?

A thought jumped into her mind. The herbs! "There were herbs that the Thorns got me to use on my dad after he was hurt. They didn't work but maybe they might have if I'd got them sooner."

Her uncle spun round. "What were they?"

Laney searched her memory. "Comfrey and vervain."

"Will you stay with her until we get back?" Her uncle rose quickly.

Laney nodded. "Yes, but where will you find the plants?"

Mr Embers didn't answer. "Tyler, I need you to come with me. Briana, find the Elder and ask him to make sure no one enters the chasm."

Stones crunched under their feet and then they were gone. Laney clambered over a boulder to get closer to her aunt. She put a hand on the cave wall to steady herself and found that the rock was warm under her fingers. The tunnel ahead stretched on into darkness and the cave floor quivered beneath her feet. It was like being inside a monster, ready to be swallowed whole.

She knelt down by her aunt and touched her hand. It was ice cold.

"Aunt Sarah?" she whispered, but her aunt didn't move.

She held her aunt's hand in the darkness and the minutes ticked by. Surely her uncle wouldn't be long? Her eyes adjusted to the gloom as she watched her aunt's still face. So the Shadow had left Skellmore. He must be looking for another Myrical. Maybe he already knew one was hidden close by.

She shivered, remembering how it felt to be struck by the Shadow's red lightning. Noticing a mark on her aunt's wrist, she pushed up the coat sleeve. A vein of blue ice ran down her aunt's arm, ending in a star-shaped burn. The Shadow's lightning must have struck right here. Laney touched the vein of ice and it melted, leaving little drops of water on her aunt's skin. Taking her aunt's arm, Laney closed her eyes and thought of fire and warmth. Little by little, her aunt grew warmer and the colour returned to her skin.

When Laney opened her eyes, the drops of water hung in the air like floating jewels. Startled, she dropped her aunt's arm. She'd used Mist magic again. But having Blaze and Mist powers at the same time wasn't supposed to be possible. Chips Delaney, who had parents from different tribes too, had reminded her of that.

She touched one of the drops as it floated in mid-air. First she'd used water magic then fire magic. Did she have *powers far apart* just like the red moon prophecy said?

There were sounds at the cave entrance. Laney snatched at the water drops, catching them in her hand and rubbing the wetness on her jeans. Her uncle and Tyler hurried up the tunnel towards them.

Her uncle gave Laney the herbs. "Do you know what you're doing?"

Laney rubbed the herbs between her hands and put them on her aunt's forehead. "This is what Gwen told me to do before. I'm not a Thorn though..."

A heavy silence fell on the cave and the only sound was water dripping from the roof. Then Laney's aunt coughed and opened her eyes. She looked around, dazed. "Connor..."

"Don't try and talk," said Mr Embers. "Just lie still."

"I remember what happened." Mrs Embers pushed herself up shakily. "I drove around the corner and he was standing by the side of the road looking towards Beggar's Chasm. His hood was low and I couldn't see his face. I was so shocked that I lost control of the car – I veered towards him – then he stretched out his hand and a tree branch smashed into my car. It was just horrible!"

"Then he must be a Thorn – or he was once," said Tyler.

"But there was ice on her arm where the lightning struck," said Laney. "And that's a Mist skill."

Tyler came forward in the gloom. "So he's a Mist or a Thorn. Now all we have to do is find everyone from those two tribes and work out who it was. Then we can nail him. We'll tell everyone—"

"No!" Mr Embers told him. "We'll tell the Elder and that's it. We don't know what's going on or why the Shadow attacked your mother."

"We don't need to know why!" Tyler yelled. "We just need to track him down and kill him."

Mr Embers faced his son. "Just think for a minute! We tell every Blaze and Greytail in the village to look for a Thorn or a Mist. What then? The only Thorn round here – half Thorn – is Christopher Delaney, and less than half an hour ago he gave us the plants that helped heal your mother. Do you want to hand him over to an angry crowd? And when they start searching for a Mist, where do you think they'll look? The only person living round here with a Mist-tribe parent is Laney."

Laney swallowed. "But if we know who the Shadow is it'll be easier to beat him."

Briana ran up the tunnel. "The Elder's here now and most of the tribe."

"Thank you, Briana. We're coming." Mr Embers gave Tyler and Laney a warning look before helping his wife to her feet.

A crowd had gathered outside the mouth of the cave.

"Everyone listen!" said Hillburn, the Blaze Elder. "If the Shadow's here, it's because there's a Myrical to be found. Our beloved Sparkstone was hidden at a time of great danger and I have long believed it must have been placed among these hills. We *must* find it before that monster does. A Shadow faerie who gets his hands on Blaze power could unleash a terrible fire, threatening many lives."

Laney shuddered. She'd seen the Shadow possess the Thorn Myrical, the Wildwood Arrow. Seeing him take the essence of Thorn magic and turn it evil had been terrifying.

"We'll begin searching at nightfall," continued the Blaze Elder. "And we'll stop anyone from another tribe who comes into this area. If they don't have a reason for being here, they won't be allowed in."

There was a murmur of agreement and the air filled with heat. Hillburn instructed the tribe to divide up and search different areas for the Myrical. Laney didn't know a lot of the places he named. She studied the determined faces around her. The natural quickness of the Blazes had transformed into a shimmering anger. They didn't seem to be afraid of the Shadow. Or maybe they just hid it well.

As soon as her aunt felt better, Laney took the herbs and persuaded Kim to drive her to the hospital. She placed the herbs on her dad's pillow and searched his face for any change – a flicker of the eyelids or a change in his breathing. Anything.

She sat by his side till sunset. Pictures ran through her head: red lightning striking her dad's chest … her aunt laying in the cave with the warm walls … the drops of water hanging in the air…

A magpie landed on a bush near the window. It was alone, which made it *"one for sorrow"* – just like the rhyme. The bird turned its head and gave a harsh squawk. Laney frowned. Why did she feel like it was staring at her?

"Laney, are you OK?" said Kim, returning from the hospital canteen with Toby.

Laney quickly put the herbs out of sight. "Yes, I

was just daydreaming."

"Well, I have some good news," Kim said brightly. "Monique Lionhart rang me. Claudia's staying at her cousin's house for a few weeks and I said we'd have her round for tea. I know it's been hard on you, moving up here. I don't want you to lose touch with your Skellmore friends."

"Thanks!" Laney beamed. Claudia was staying in Kirkfield at last! But would her mum take her straight back to Skellmore when she found out the Shadow had been seen?

Kim walked over to the bed and touched her husband on the cheek. Laney noticed how worried she looked. "He's worse instead of better, isn't he?" she said.

"The doctors said he might have ups and downs," Kim replied. "But he's in the right place and he's got experts looking after him. Come on, you're just tired. Get your things and we'll go."

Kim filled the silence in the car, talking about the news Simon had brought from Skellmore. Although her stepmum knew nothing of the faerie world, Laney could tell a lot from what she relayed. Injured cats. Broken trees. It was clear the tribes were still fighting each other, especially the Greytails and the Thorns.

They picked up Claudia from her cousin's house in Kirkfield and then carried on to Little Shackle.

Laney knew from Claudia's meaningful look that she had heard about the Shadow's attack in the village, and as soon as the two girls were alone, back at Laney's house, she demanded information.

"I knew there must be a Myrical hidden in this area!" Claudia said when Laney had finished telling her everything.

"I don't remember you saying that before," Laney replied.

Claudia brushed this off. "Course I did." She leaned in. "And by the way, there's someone listening at your window." She whirled round, snapped the window open and grabbed Tyler's arm, pulling him in backwards.

"Ow! Watch it!" Tyler collapsed on the floor, his dark-red wings crooked. "How did you know I was there?"

Claudia raised one eyebrow. "You can't spy on a Greytail. We have sharper senses than anyone. I could have heard you a mile away."

"This is Tyler, my cousin," Laney told her. "Tyler, what were you doing outside my window – don't you trust me or something?"

Tyler shifted back to human form. "Yeah, I trust *you*. I don't trust her though. Everyone knows Greytails only care about themselves."

"Everyone knows Blazes are really moody and stink of smoke," replied Claudia.

"Stop it – both of you!" said Laney. "Tyler, tell me why you were outside my window."

"We have to check all the new people coming into the village. And she's new!" Tyler said.

"You're lying! I can tell by the way you won't look us in the eye," Claudia snapped. "Anyway, the Greytails living here have already told your Elder all about me."

"OK, fine! The truth is I just came to say thanks," Tyler said to Laney. "It was lucky you knew what to do to help my mum. It was horrible seeing her injured. It made me think about how hard things have been for you with your dad so ill." He met Laney's eyes. "So I came to ask you how he is. If there's anything I can do to help, I will."

CHAPTER
11

That night the Blazes began searching for the Sparkstone. They took candles lit with pale-blue flames into the hills. These gave off enough light to search by but were hard to spot from the village below. Laney wanted to help but she was told they had plenty of people. From listening to their conversations, she realised they were concentrating their Myrical hunt on the hills and the caves beneath them. She thought of the cave at Beggar's Chasm and wondered how far it stretched under the hills.

Claudia settled in at her cousin's house and she and Laney met up quite often in Kirkfield. March turned into April and the days at school dragged by. The scent of warm earth filled the air and Mrs McKee from next door was in her garden every day, planting vegetables. Buds appeared on the branches of the trees and daffodils opened on the roadsides. Laney watched them nodding their golden heads as Kim drove her to school each morning.

Shafts of sunlight lit up Groaning Tor by day. Amber light flickered on the peak by night. Laney thought of the story of the giant hidden underneath the hill. Every evening, she sneaked into the field behind their cottage after Kim had gone to bed and practised Blaze skills in the dark. Sometimes she conjured up flames over and over until her hands were sore. At first her fireballs vanished in mid-air and her circles of fire were just wobbly lines. But as the weeks went by, she got better until even Tyler admitted that she was doing well.

Maybe if she could pass the test on the night of the Kindling and become a proper Blaze, everything else would be all right too: her dad would wake up, he'd be well again and they'd all be together. If only she could get the fire magic right. She longed to tell her dad about her Blaze powers. She wanted to see that look in his eye that told her he was proud of her.

"Show me how to make the frost flames again," she said to Tyler. "I can never get them cold enough."

They were practising in the field behind Laney's cottage again. The sun had set, leaving a thin line of gold on the horizon.

"It's easy!" Tyler clicked his fingers and a flame lit in his hand as pure white as a burning icicle. "Don't let the fire burst out like you do with a normal flame; just keep it small and tight."

Laney wrinkled her forehead. "Sure – no problem! Except that's what I've tried to do the last fifty million times."

"Great, more Blaze practice!" Claudia yawned, perching on top of the fence. "Don't you think it's weird that you don't burn your own hands? It's like you're flame-proofed or something."

Tyler's frost flame shot upwards, turning his fringe white. "Where did you spring from?"

Claudia grinned. "I've been sitting here for five minutes."

"It's a Greytail stealth thing," Laney told him. "You get used to it. I didn't know you were coming over tonight, Claudia."

"My mum dropped me off. She, Gwen and Frogley are having some kind of super-important meeting with the Blaze Elders." Claudia stifled another yawn. "They're all in the village right now."

Laney bit her lip. She knew the Skellmore Elders had visited Little Shackle a couple of times since she'd moved here. They'd probably come to talk about the search for the Myricals. She hoped she didn't run into Frogley. The Mist Elder was always horrible to her.

"Come on, Laney," Tyler said impatiently. "Try making that frost flame."

"OK hold on." Laney clicked her fingers and concentrated on making a really small flame. For a second she thought it would burn yellow but it leapt up small, cold and white. Her stomach turned over. The flame felt icy cold on her skin.

Tyler grinned. "Finally! A frost flame."

Claudia shuddered. "Yuck! At least normal fire keeps you warm." A small black cat jumped on to the fence beside her and mewed. "See, Dizzy agrees with me. So, you crazy fire people haven't had any luck at finding your Myrical then."

"Mind your own business." Tyler glared at her.

Claudia swung down from the fence, suddenly tense. "Watch out – someone's coming."

A minute later, Frogley walked into the field. He was followed by Tyler's dad, who wore a troubled look on his face. "I don't see why you need to speak to my niece," he said to the Mist Elder. "It's not as if she's from your tribe."

Frogley smiled thinly. "No, she isn't! Apparently the whole of Little Shackle knows she's a Blaze faerie even though she was coming to Mist training sessions back in Skellmore." His eyes glinted as he turned to Laney. "I shall be telling everyone how you pretended to be part of our tribe. What do you think they'll say about you then?"

"I wasn't pretending!" Laney told him. "I didn't know I was a Blaze back then."

"How can you not know what you are?" Frogley's cold eyes flicked to Tyler. "I wonder what your new family have to say about that."

Laney's heart sank. Tyler was looking confused. What would her uncle, aunt and cousin think of how she tried to join the Mists back in Skellmore? Would they start doubting whether she should be allowed into the Blaze tribe?

Frogley smiled at her silence. "All you are is a liar and a Tainted."

"That's enough!" Laney's uncle clapped a hand on

Frogley's shoulder. "You've said your piece. Now, go before I make you leave!"

Frogley shrugged his hand off. "She Awakened on the night of a red moon. Did she tell you that?"

Laney paled. A red moon, sometimes called a wolf moon, was the most frightening omen in the faerie world. No one else knew the secret she'd discovered just before she left Skellmore – that her dad had hidden the truth about the date she was born. He'd told everyone she had a different birthday and changed the date on her birth certificate. She hadn't just Awakened on the night of a red moon, she'd been born on one too. The words of the prophecy started running through her head:

Born under a Wolf Moon
The Child of Aether joins together powers far apart.
He binds the opposites
And drives a splinter through the faerie ring's heart.

But all that couldn't be about her, could it?

Frogley smiled as if he knew he'd won the argument. Laney's uncle stepped towards the Mist Elder, but Frogley turned and hurried back to the road.

"Nasty little man!" Mr Embers said, watching Frogley go. "If he bothers you again just let me know, Laney."

Tyler folded his arms. "I can always get rid of him for you. He only has water magic after all."

"Thanks!" Laney smiled.

"Laney, I'd like you to come home with us," added her uncle. "There's something I want to say to you. Claudia, I'll show you where your mum will meet you to take you home."

Laney felt an uneasy wriggling in her stomach as she and Tyler followed Mr Embers back to Tinder Street. Did her uncle want to talk about what Frogley had said?

Mr Embers let them into the house and closed the red front door firmly behind them. "Come and sit by the fire a minute," he said. "Tyler, put the kettle on and tell your mother we're back. She always worries."

For once Tyler didn't argue.

Laney sat in the armchair by the fire. Her heart sank as she looked at her uncle, who was now searching through a cupboard. "Is this about the red moon prophecy?" She hesitated. Did her uncle know about her real birthday?

Mr Embers took out a pile of papers and sat opposite her. "I know your dad changed the date on your birth certificate," he told her. "But he only told his closest relatives. Lots of people are superstitious about those that are born on the night of a red moon but no one knows if that prophecy really means anything. That's not what I wanted to talk to you about."

"Oh." Laney's heart stopped thudding so fast.

"Don't worry about Frogley either," he added gruffly. "None of us trust him. We can all see he's a slippery kind of man. He's a Mist and – well, your father was the only dependable Mist I've ever met. Each tribe has their faults, I suppose. Anyway I wanted to give you these." He held out the papers he'd taken from the cupboard. "I looked them out a few days ago. I know your father left nearly everything behind that night you came here, so *The Wind in the Willows* book is probably the only thing that you have of Cordelia's. These were hers too – they're things she did as a child."

Tyler came through from the kitchen and set three mugs of tea down on the table.

"Oh, thank you!" Laney took the papers eagerly and began looking through them. They were a collection of childish pictures drawn with a wobbly hand and coloured in with crayons, and a story written in an old exercise book. Laney paused over a drawing of a river with purple and white flowers along the edge. There were ducks on the water.

"When we were growing up the other kids would say she wasn't normal," said Mr Embers. "The things she liked and the things she said – they were different from everyone else. I fought all the boys that picked on her until she told me to stop. *Don't bother, Connor,* she said. *Their names can never hurt me. They just trickle away like water.* She seemed to love the things most Blazes don't like at all."

"Like rivers?" Laney looked from her uncle to the picture.

Mr Embers smiled. "She loved that brook. It's a couple of miles out of the village on the Kirkfield road. One summer she spent a whole week paddling up and down it catching little fish. She brought some of them home once but our parents wouldn't let her keep them."

Laney put the papers down on her lap. "I guess they weren't pleased about her marrying a Mist either." Her uncle didn't reply. Laney decided she had to ask him now, while she felt brave enough. "The night my mum died and my dad brought me here ... he always told me she got ill. But that's not true, is it? Someone killed her."

Mr Embers sighed deeply and rubbed his beard. "It shouldn't really be me that tells you ... but with Robert in hospital..." He stared at the fire for a while and then at last he spoke. "I only know the bare facts as your father told them to me. Your parents left Little Shackle because they knew their marriage would not be accepted here. We heard little from them for more than two years. It was an awful time, under the threat of the Great Shadow.

People turned on each other, suspecting anyone who showed any sign of being different. Your mother and father were right to run away – I just wish leaving here had saved her."

The fire crackled in the grate as he continued. "Cordelia died in a lightning strike. Robert said he didn't know how they'd been discovered. He never saw the face of the faerie who threw the bolt that killed her."

Laney's throat tightened painfully. "I remember a little bit of that night. I can picture standing at your door and my dad was holding something – like a purse."

Her uncle nodded. "It was her dust. That was all he managed to save – your mother's dust. He gave it to me so that I could bury it here, where she came from. But even then, the Elders of that time wouldn't let me bury her here in Little Shackle because she'd married a Mist, so I had to put her to rest up in Beggar's Chasm near the faerie ring."

"My mum's buried up there?"

"Yes. She loved it there. She said she liked the peace and quiet, with the noise of the stream and the birds flying over the chasm. When this hunt for the Myrical is over I'll take you up there and show you the exact spot." The firelight shone over her uncle's face.

"At least your dad saved her dust," Tyler said. "It

would've been horrible if he hadn't."

Laney knew what he meant. She hadn't forgotten the day that Mr Willowby died and the Shadow stole his body to use in dark magic. "I think I understand now why my dad never wanted me to Awaken," she said. "I used to think he didn't want me to be free." Her eyes stung.

"This new Shadow will regret the day he came to Little Shackle," Mr Embers said grimly. "Too often we've hidden from these monsters that use faerie's dust for their spells. But no more. This time we fight back. The moment he struck at my Sarah, he guaranteed his downfall."

Looking from Tyler to her uncle, Laney saw the same grim determined expression. Her fingers curled around the crayon picture of ducks on a river, drawn so many years ago by a strange Blaze girl who loved water. "I'll do anything I can to help," she told them. "It's time I started fighting back too."

CHAPTER
12

After learning how to make a frost flame, Laney's Blaze skills grew stronger day by day. Soon she could make rings of fire that burned for several minutes, and hit a target on the other side of the field with her fireballs. As she lobbed the balls of flame, she pictured the Shadow on the day he'd hurt her dad.

Next time she'd be ready to fight him.

The day of the Kindling wasn't far away. Preparations began, away from the eyes of the humans. Logs were gathered and hidden in the hills. Branches were chopped from hawthorn hedges and the stems woven into arches. Covered with new leaves and white blossom, the arches reminded Laney of something out of an old-fashioned country wedding rather than a ceremony of fire. When she helped take the hawthorn arches up to Groaning Tor, she saw Briana doing the same. The other girl ignored her as they passed. It was obvious she didn't think Laney should be included.

There was a lot of talk about the Bale Fire and Laney asked Tyler what it was but he was annoyingly mysterious. "You'll see. Just make sure you've told your stepmum a good excuse – the Kindling lasts all night."

So Laney told Kim she'd be staying with Claudia in Kirkfield that night.

"Are you all right, Laney?" Kim came into Laney's

room just as she was getting ready to leave for the Kindling.

"I'm fine." Laney couldn't admit she felt nervous.

"It's just that you've been so quiet lately." Kim's forehead creased. "I know everything's been difficult but if there's anything you want to talk about…"

"Honestly, I'm fine." Guilt tightened Laney's stomach. She hated not being honest with Kim about where she was going. "I mean, it's been hard with Dad ill but I'm glad we came to Little Shackle. You were right – it would've been horrible to be far away from him."

Kim hugged her. "We'll get through this like we always do! Have a lovely time tonight."

Laney sighed after Kim shut the door. She'd got used to hiding the faerie world from her stepmum but she needed to tell her about finding her uncle and aunt. Kim had been good to her for so long. She promised herself she'd do it once this Kindling was over.

As darkness fell, Laney took out her mum's writing and drawings. She'd read the story written in the old exercise book every day since her uncle had given it to her. It was about a rabbit who found a cave behind a waterfall. The story ended with the rabbit learning to swim, which made Laney smile. It was strange to think of her mum as a little girl making up her rabbit story, but Laney also felt it helped her know her mum a little better. She put the papers back in their hiding place and went out to meet Tyler.

They left the village and took the path to Groaning Tor, passing Blazes who were guarding the hillside, there to stop anyone outside the tribe from stumbling upon the celebrations. The peak – so pale in the daytime – flickered with orange sparks as if fire was bubbling up inside. Laney suddenly wondered if there were flames down there. "Tyler, what's underneath Groaning Tor?" she asked. "And don't tell me it's a giant."

Tyler grinned. "Wait and see!"

As they scrambled to the top, a shining white circle sailed out from behind a bank of clouds. It cast ghostly moonlight across the boulders and the rolling hills.

"It's good that there's a full moon this year," Tyler said. "It'll make the Blaze magic stronger."

A large crowd had gathered on the plateau beyond the peak. Violins and flutes were playing a jig and lots of people were dancing. The drums beat a rhythm that pulsed through Laney's head. There was a wildness in the music beyond happiness or sadness. It reminded Laney of how she'd felt when she'd used her wings for the first time. A feeling so bright it could burn you.

Mr Embers clasped Laney on the shoulder. "Welcome to your first Kindling!" he smiled broadly. "The Blaze Elder will light the Bale Fire and then you and the other Learners will have a chance to show what you can do."

Laney's stomach dropped. Had she really done enough practice? What if she couldn't even light a flame?

Tyler grinned and yelled into her ear. "Stop looking so worried! Your frost flames are just as good as mine. You *are* ready!"

"Quiet!" The shout from the Blaze Elder pierced through the noise and the music came to a halt. "At midnight, the first of May will dawn – the beginning of the Blaze year. We have much to be thankful for and also much we need to do." His gaze swept the crowd. "Bring forward the May tree arches and I will light the Bale Fire."

People came forward with the arches of blossom and hawthorn. They made a circle around Hillburn, lining up their arches to make a leafy tunnel. The Elder took one branch up to the peak. He tapped three times on the rock and the ground shook beneath their feet. Then a jet of golden flame surged out of the hole in the rock and burned like a torch.

"The giant's awake!" yelled some of the Blazes.

Hillburn lit the branch in the golden flame and carried it back to the circle. Then he used it to light the May tree arches and each one burned with a luminous silver flame. A buzz went round the crowd.

Laney jumped as Tyler spoke into her ear, more quietly this time. "The silver flame's a good sign. If the Kindling goes well then we'll have good luck this year."

"But the branches aren't burning," Laney whispered back. "I mean – they're not burning into nothing."

"Bale Fire doesn't destroy things," Tyler grinned. "It's like magic!"

It was pretty amazing seeing the arches alight while the leaves and blossoms stayed untouched, and the silvery Bale Fire was beautiful. Laney felt her courage rise. Maybe she would be able to show them all her Blaze skills. On a night like this anything seemed possible.

The music began to play again and people went through the arches. Mrs Embers was one of the first to walk through, helped by her husband. Laney knew her aunt had struggled since the Shadow had struck her car. After passing through the arch she seemed to walk a little straighter.

"Come on!" Tyler grabbed her arm and they raced in and out of the arches.

Laney felt weightless. The drum beat echoed through her body and she changed to faerie form without really noticing. The music swirled around the hill and the people whirled with it. Laney felt her feet lift off the ground. Many of the Blazes were now flying over the Tor and swooping down to dip through the arches. The shining white-faced moon watched over the celebrations. The melody grew faster and faster until it finished on a great crescendo that left everyone floating back to earth, laughing.

"Well now!" Hillburn gazed round with a great beaming smile. "Excellent playing!" The musicians gave a bow. "Now let's have our younger ones show us their skills."

Laney knew this was her moment. She went to the centre of the circle with three younger children. One of the others went first, giving Laney a chance to steady her nerves. She tried to remember all the things she and Tyler had practised in the field behind her cottage.

"When you're ready, Elaine." Hillburn nodded to her.

Laney's stomach turned over. This was it. Fire burst out of her so easily when it shouldn't, so why was it so hard to produce the rest of the time? She lifted her hands and Tyler's words flashed through her mind. *The flame doesn't come from your hand – not really. It comes from inside you.*

She thought of the fire inside and a small flame

sprang up in her palm. She held it steady. It was working! She was really doing it!

She pushed her excitement down and kept her eyes fixed on the flame. The next step was to use it to make a ring of fire. She needed to take her other hand and draw the circle. Her arms felt heavy as if she'd forgotten how to move them. She mustn't panic – she knew what to do.

A dark breeze swept across the hilltop and the moonlight dimmed. Laney's skin prickled but she ignored it. Raising her hand, she dipped her fingers in the flame and drew the circle of fire above her head. The first part was wobbly but she carried on, keeping her hand as steady as she could. When the ring was complete she stood back to check it. Then she looked over at her uncle, expecting a smile. But he wasn't looking at her at all.

Every face was turned to the sky and the crowd buzzed with alarm. Laney looked up, wondering what the matter was. Had someone from a different tribe invaded the ceremony? What if it were Frogley?

But there was no one there. The sky was empty except for the moon. That great white-faced moon.

Except it didn't have a white face any more. It was slowly changing colour – darkening into something else...

It was turning red.

"The Wolf Moon!" The shout went up from the crowd.

The moon gradually changed to a dark-red disc. The colour of blood.

Laney's heart turned cold. It was happening again. That awful night when she'd Awakened. Even before she'd found out about the prophecy and the fears of the tribes, she'd known there was something horribly wrong about a moon like this. Something evil.

"Everyone stay exactly where you are," said the Blaze Elder.

"Look at the Bale Fire," screamed Briana.

A new cry of horror burst from the people on the hill. The arches of Bale Fire no longer burned a beautiful silver. The flames were darkening to red, echoing the colour of the moon.

"It's her!" Briana pointed at Laney. "She was making a spell when it started. She's bad luck!"

"I didn't do anything," Laney cried.

Briana met her gaze and Laney could see the other girl didn't believe her.

"Quiet, everyone!" the Blaze Elder commanded. "This is our place and our Kindling. We will *not* forget ourselves." Once everyone was silent, he returned to the golden flame burning from the crevice in the Tor. Lighting another branch, he took it to each of the arches in turn.

The hillside held its breath.

Laney tried to ignore the hollow feeling inside. Why had the moon turned red right at the moment she'd tried to prove her Blaze magic? It couldn't have been her. She didn't have that kind of power.

Hillburn tried over and over but the golden flame didn't change the blood-stained fire on the arches. Rain started to fall, whipped into the faces of the crowd by a spiteful wind.

Laney's circle of fire had vanished from the air. "Do you want me to try the circle again?" she faltered. The faces around her looked grim.

Tyler broke through the front of the crowd. "This was nothing to do with her. I've watched her practise – I've been helping her – and her spells were totally fine."

"She must've been faking it," Zac called out. Next to him, Callum was nodding.

"Don't be an idiot! I'd have known if she was faking it." Tyler clenched his fists. "Or are you saying I'm not enough of a Blaze to work it out?"

"Tyler, wait!" Laney turned to the Elder. "I really didn't do this. You believe me, don't you?" She could already see the answer in his eyes.

"Maybe the red moon isn't your fault, but either way I think you should leave," Hillburn said heavily. "I don't believe in persecuting someone because of who their mother married – the cruel ways of the past are behind us – but there's something wrong here. We must protect our Bale Fire and the essence of our magic above all things."

"You need to make sure the tribe doesn't get *tainted*, right? That's what the name means – that I could infect you all – like I'm a germ or something." Laney choked back a sob. "This wasn't me." She gestured at the red moon. "And you're right; there *is* something wrong here because none of you can bring yourselves to trust someone who's different from you."

Laney ran into the darkness. She heard some of the Blazes calling for her to be stopped and Hillburn telling them to let her go. She walked for a while before realising she was going further into the hills instead of back to Little Shackle. She didn't even know where she was. The whole place was flooded with red moonlight, like a nightmare turned real.

Scanning the hillside, Laney searched for a path to take her downhill. She went along a rough track, emerging from between two boulders to find a strange red fog creeping down the slope. Tendrils of orange-red mist curled round her ankles. There was something familiar about it... That was it – she'd seen the same kind of reddish fog on the night she'd Awakened. There'd been a red moon that night too.

Laney waded through the fog for several minutes. She hated touching the horrible, clammy stuff. She had no idea where she was, and the fog was getting thicker. She stumbled into a small hollow and her heart froze. Crouching on the ground was a dark figure in a black cloak and hood. In his hands was a small purse embroidered with snowdrops – the same purse Mrs Willowby had used to collect her husband's dust after he died all those months ago in Skellmore.

As Laney watched in horror, specks of dust whirled out of the purse into the air, where they vanished into the reddish fog, which matched the colour of the moon exactly. Laney's breath caught in her throat. This was a shadow spell – dark magic created by using a dead faerie's dust. It was so strong it was turning the moon red.

The Shadow turned his head as if he sensed she was there. Laney ran. Red lightning arced around her. Then a second bolt struck the ground close by, searing a jagged mark across the grass.

Laney raced on, desperate to get away. Stumbling forwards, her foot met nothing as the ground jerked away beneath her. She plunged into the earth, bashing her head against rock and tumbling several feet before smashing into a hard stone floor. Darkness danced in front of her eyes. Trembling, she pulled herself over to the rocky wall and leaned against it. Her forehead throbbed like mad and when she touched it her hand came away wet with blood. It probably wasn't a very big cut, she told herself, but she couldn't stop shaking.

Where was she?

The moon was like a red searchlight, shining on the narrow gash in the rock through which she'd fallen. A dark figure swooped overhead and Laney shrank into the gloom. The Shadow was out there looking for her. The red moon was created by his shadow spell, she was sure of it. He was probably using magic to try and find the Myricals – that was what he always wanted.

She leaned her head against the rock. She wanted to go back to the Blaze tribe and explain that the red moon wasn't her fault. But would they even listen?

She lit a flame and it spluttered in her shaking hand. Now she could see more of the hole she'd fallen into. To her left, it widened into a tunnel that stretched on into darkness. Her head ached so much from hitting it as she fell that she wasn't sure she could make it back to Little Shackle. She wasn't even sure she had the strength to change into faerie form.

Letting the flame go out, she began crawling across the rough ground. The ceiling was too low to stand up at first so she was glad to reach a cave with a higher roof and a smooth earth floor. She lay down, feeling the warmth of the earth against her back. Images circled around her pounding head – the Bale Fire, the faces of the Blaze tribe, Tyler pushing to the front of the crowd. The pain dulled a little and she started to doze.

She woke with a start. Or was she still dreaming?

Two small green lights gleamed in the darkness.

Laney sat up fast, heart thumping. A flame sprang up in her hand. The fire lit up a small black shape around the green lights. The green glow blinked out for a second and then reappeared.

"Dizzy!" Laney smiled in relief at the little cat.

"Did Claudia send you to find me? Does she know I'm down here?"

The cat ignored the questions and began to wash. There was a faint padding noise and another cat joined her – a sleek tortoiseshell with sharp amber eyes. Laney had the strange feeling she'd seen those eyes before. The tortoiseshell sat on its haunches and watched her intently.

"Is this your friend, Dizzy?" Laney asked.

Dizzy stopped washing and looked at Laney as if she was mad.

The tortoiseshell yawned and stretched, and kept on stretching. Its limbs shimmered and thickened and its fur smoothed into human skin. Within a few moments, the cat had transformed completely and Claudia sat on the cave floor in her jeans and T-shirt. Dizzy gave her a look and went back to washing.

"Flippin' heck!" Laney stared at her friend. "How did you do that? You never told me you could do that!"

"I only learned this spring." Claudia sprang to her feet. "And we're not supposed to tell Greytail secrets."

"Oh." Laney tried to stop staring. She supposed it made sense that changing into an animal was a Greytail thing. "Can you change into anything you like?"

"Just a cat. Some Greytails manage wolves." Claudia blinked. Her eyes still had the same quick-thinking look even though she'd changed. "Using cat form was the only way I could get up here. The whole place is crawling with Blazes and they're all talking about you. Why do they blame you for the red moon? What did you do?"

"Nothing, I swear! I was just beginning to show them what I've been practising and the moon changed colour out of nowhere. Then when I ran away, I saw the Shadow using dust to make a spell. It was horrible!"

Claudia looked alarmed. "The Shadow's here! Then we should keep moving."

Laney looked down the tunnel. "You came from that direction – does that mean there's another way out?"

"Loads of them! These tunnels run for miles under these hills. The local Greytails have told me about them. They don't come down here though. It's strictly Blaze territory."

A low rumble echoed through the tunnel, as though the earth was groaning. Laney put her hand to the cave wall and found it was warm. "They have a legend that there's a fire giant down here. This is a special place for Blazes. They'll hate me being down here after what happened."

"Well, I'm getting out of here," said Claudia.

"I hate caves and there's a good chance both the Shadow *and* the Blazes are looking for you."

Dizzy arched her back and gave a faint hiss. Laney heard low voices coming from the tunnel where she'd fallen in. Claudia put a finger to her lips and crept to the opposite end of the cave, vanishing into a fold in the rock. Laney followed her and found there was a small vertical crack. She squeezed through sideways and Dizzy slipped in behind. They were in a long tunnel and Laney had to bend her neck to avoid the low cave roof.

There was a crash from behind. "They sound like elephants!" muttered Claudia. "They're in the tunnels – two adults, I think."

A coil of flame snaked into the cavern they'd just left. It circled the floor like it was searching for prey and then curled back to where it had come from.

The girls fled along the tunnel. Laney tried to tread lightly like Claudia but felt she was crunching on every loose stone. Stopping behind a stalagmite pillar, she caught her breath. No ribbons of flame followed them but there was a faint glow in the direction they'd come from. Laney decided to risk it and light a small flame of her own. The sudden view of the cave made her shudder. The tunnel had widened out. She'd guessed that already as every noise echoed a little more. What she hadn't expected was the sheer drop a few steps to the right where the cave floor fell away. The bottom was hidden in darkness.

"Did you know that was there?" she asked Claudia.

"Course." Claudia raised an eyebrow. "It's not as deep as it looks. Don't worry; I wouldn't have let you fall."

Laney had to look away as it was making her stomach twist. Her flame sputtered. The light flickered on the cluster of stalactites plunging from the cave ceiling.

"Weird place." Claudia ran her fingers over one of the rock pillars. "It's funny that they're warm. I thought everything would be cold down here."

Dizzy ran towards a large rock, mewing, and Tyler came out from behind it. "You shouldn't be down here, either of you. The tribe's looking for you, Laney."

"I don't *want* to be down here," said Claudia, rolling her eyes. "Now you've found us you can show us the quickest way out."

"I'll try but there are things—" Tyler broke off as a rumbling sound echoed round the cave.

Laney grabbed a column of rock to steady herself. "I saw the Shadow," she told Tyler. "I'm sure he was the one that made the red moon."

"He was up here on the hillside?" Tyler looked shocked.

"He wasn't far away from where the Kindling was happening," Laney said. "We have to warn everyone."

Tyler ran off and Laney and Claudia raced after him, with Dizzy at their feet. Laney tried to keep the flame in her hand alight. She wasn't going to risk falling down any chasms in these caves.

Tyler stopped short where the passageway split into three, his hand resting on the cave wall. The air coming from the right-hand tunnel was hot and dry like a desert wind. Maybe the Blazes had lit a fire that way. Laney felt something tugging inside her. She longed to go down that tunnel more than anything. Her pulse raced. Why did she want to go down there so much?

Suddenly everything fell into place.

"It's down here, isn't it?" Laney said to Tyler.

"What's down here?" Claudia frowned.

"I should have realised!" Laney said. "All those patrols – all the people searching the hills and tunnels. Except they were only pretending to search because all of you already knew where the Blaze Myrical was."

"Laney!" Tyler flicked a warning look at Claudia.

Laney lowered her voice. "You've got the Sparkstone hidden in here! You've probably kept it safe for years. I'm right, aren't I? All that stuff about a fire giant under the hill was just a cover … and that's why the caves are so warm." Tyler's face told her she was right. "None of you trusted me enough to tell me because I'm a Tainted."

"We had to keep it a secret, especially with the Shadow around." Tyler put a hand on her shoulder. "Don't be angry. At least you're going to see it now!"

As they ran, Laney felt like something was drawing her down the tunnel – making her feet move faster. The essence of Blaze magic was gathered in the Sparkstone and she was finally going to see it. She was sure it would be beautiful. She, Claudia and Tyler followed the zigzag of the passageway. Tyler lit a flame too and the lights bobbed as they ran. They were running so fast that they were almost on top of the still figure before they saw it.

"Wait!" Laney's shout pulled her friends to a halt. "It's Briana!"

Briana seemed to be stuck to the tunnel wall. She was motionless, her eyes shut. Dark smoke weaved around her legs and arms, rising to her neck and curling round her red hair. Her face was as pale as death. Horrified, Laney watched the ceaseless whirling of the smoke. This was a Shadow spell. She'd seen this kind of thing before.

"Briana!" Tyler reached out for her.

"Don't touch the smoke, Tyler!" Laney said. "It's Shadow magic and it will hurt you."

A tendril of smoke curled lazily towards them

and Dizzy hissed at it, her fur standing on end.

"I don't care about getting hurt!" Tyler exploded. "Briana, can you hear me?"

Briana didn't stir. Her body rested stiffly against the wall, her arms hanging by her sides.

Claudia shivered. "The Shadow's down here then. We should keep moving."

Tyler clenched his fists. "We have to find a way to break the spell. We need the right herbs like we did for my mum when she was hurt."

"I don't know if that'll work this time. This spell looks strong. We should find your dad and tell him what's happened," Laney said. "If the Shadow's down here, no one is safe."

CHAPTER
14

Tyler stared at Briana frozen against the tunnel wall. "We can't just leave her."

"I don't want to either but we've got no choice!" Laney said. "Tyler, come on. We've got to tell your dad. Maybe Hillburn will be able to free her from the spell."

Tyler shook himself out of indecision. "There should be people guarding the Myrical. It's not far now!"

As they ran on the air grew hotter, scorching Laney's throat as she breathed. The heat baked her skin, and her clothes – damp from the earlier rain – dried fast. They passed another figure immobilised on the tunnel floor. Little wisps of black smoke circled him too.

"It's Zac." Tyler's fists clenched and fire burned between his fingers.

Claudia looked back. "Don't stop. There's something behind us."

They raced on in silence and the heat in the tunnel lessened a little, making it easier to run.

"It's here." Tyler got down on hands and knees to get through a gap in the wall.

Laney crawled through next, emerging into a cavern lit with soft white light which poured from a pillar of rock in the centre. A million flecks of quartz glittered on the walls and ceiling like tiny distant stars. Laney held out her hands to the light.

It felt like warm water washing over her skin. The Sparkstone must be there, inside the huge stalagmite. No wonder the Blazes had chosen to keep it safe here under the ground.

Claudia emerged through the gap with Dizzy. "Where are all the Blazes?"

Laney's heart quickened. "I don't know." There was a strange patch of darkness at the side of the cave. She could see it with the corner of her eye.

"The light's weaker than I remember." Tyler moved closer to the pillar.

Laney wanted to follow but instead she forced herself to look at the cave's edge. For a moment, she was sure that the patch of darkness was nothing strange after all. Then with one smooth movement, the darkness collected into a cloaked figure with huge black wings. The Shadow glided into the light with red lightning crackling at his fingertips. His black hood hung low, hiding his face, and the stench of rotten things drifted across the cavern.

"We're too late." Laney's legs trembled.

"Yes, you're *much* too late," sneered the Shadow. "And yet for me your timing is perfect because now I can show you the killing of the Sparkstone and the destruction of all Blaze power, including your own. All you have to do is watch."

"Go!" Claudia hissed at Dizzy and the cat sprang for the tunnel.

The Shadow shot red lightning at Dizzy but missed and a black scorch line marked the cave floor. "Doesn't matter!" He gave a harsh laugh. "Your animals won't be able to help you." He opened one gloved hand and released a wave of black smoke that enveloped the pillar full of light.

Tyler lit a ball of flame and hurled it at the Shadow, who deflected it with a wave of his hand.

"Laney, help me!" Tyler lit another ball and another.

Laney made a frost flame in her hand, tall and ice sharp.

The Shadow beat off Tyler's fireballs, before launching black smoke at the boy. It spiralled round Tyler's legs, pinning him to the spot. Laney struck at the Shadow with her frost flame but he snatched it from her and sent it spinning to the edge of the cavern.

Then he knocked her to the ground. "Your Tainted magic is weak – infected by your mixed-tribe parents." He released another cloud of smoke, this time towards Claudia.

"Claudia, run!" cried Laney.

Claudia shut her eyes, her face tensing as the smoke twisted round her. Then her body shimmered and grew shorter until she was a quick-eyed tortoiseshell cat crouching on the cave floor. The cat bared its teeth at the Shadow and fled.

"That's the Greytails, loyal to the end." The Shadow sounded amused. "But I only need you, Tainted girl. After the way you burned me last autumn it's only right that you should be the one to help destroy this Stone." He waved a hand and the smoke twisting around Tyler thickened.

"I'll never do that!" Laney kept her voice steady. "Not after the way you hurt my dad."

"He shouldn't have married a Blaze," hissed the Shadow. "It's an offence against nature! Crimes like that must be punished and now he's got what he deserves."

Laney's panic hardened into fury. This Shadow had taken her dad away. She didn't care how dangerous it was – she'd fought him before and this time she had fire magic. She opened her hand, expecting her anger to send flames leaping up high but the fire in her palm fluttered weakly, like a butterfly's wings.

"Laney!" Tyler whispered. The smoke spiralled round his chest and rose to his neck. He could barely move his mouth now and his head was tilted at a strange angle. He flicked his eyes sideways and Laney followed his gaze. The black smoke around the central pillar had thickened too. It swirled faster, drawing up dust from the ground like a tornado. The beautiful white light inside grew dimmer. Slowly, its glow faded until finally it blinked and died.

The only light left came from the tiny phosphorescent rocks overhead. Laney's legs shook. How could dark magic smother the Sparkstone so easily? The Shadow must have grown even stronger.

"This is your part, girl," the Shadow told her. "Reach in and touch the pillar. The Myrical will come to you because you're a Blaze – well, half a Blaze."

"No!" Laney backed away.

The Shadow gripped her shoulder with a hand like ice and pushed her closer to the pillar. The rotting smell from his cloak filled her nostrils and her shoulder grew numb as cold spread through her skin and into her bones. "Take the stone! Or I shall strike the boy with lightning."

Laney's eyes flew to Tyler, frozen like a statue. She had to protect him. But the Sparkstone was sacred to the Blazes and in the Shadow's hands its power could be deadly. "If you want it, take it yourself!"

The Shadow gripped Laney's shoulder even tighter and her head started to spin. "TAKE the stone!" He sent a bolt of lightning zigzagging across the cave floor. It hit Tyler's foot and the toe of his trainer melted a little. Tyler's face didn't twitch. Laney could see that he was now completely paralysed by the Shadow's spell.

"OK, stop! I'll do it!" She reached into the smoke

surrounding the pillar and it pricked her skin like hundreds of needles. When her fingers met the pillar they slid into the rock, as if the hard surface had turned to jelly at her touch. Her hand closed around a smooth glass-like object.

"Take it quickly or my spell will freeze you," the Shadow ordered.

Laney pulled the stone and it came away easily. As soon as her arm was free from the spell smoke, the terrible prickling stopped. The Sparkstone lay heavily in her hand, a smoky-grey crystal with a long flat shape. The edges were angular and each side gave a glimpse of its nearly hidden centre, like doors to the power within.

Holding it tight, Laney wrenched herself from the Shadow's grip and fought to make a flame. Now she had the Sparkstone she had to use it. She wished for as much fire as the stone could give her – tall, billowing flames of gold and red – but the Sparkstone remained cold and the fire didn't come.

"Burn!" she told it desperately. "Please!" Surely the Shadow's spell hadn't been powerful enough to crush all the Blaze power in the stone. There had to be a tiny glimmer of magic left.

"You have lost this fight," said the Shadow. "I will keep this Myrical. My ally, the White Shadow of the north, will take the Greytail and Kestrel Myricals and together we will rule over all the faerie tribes.

Once the Mist and Thorn Myricals are released from where you and that Whitefern woman hid them for a year and a day, we'll take them too."

Laney shivered. The Shadow had spoken of another dark faerie once before. She held on to the Sparkstone tightly. Why hadn't he tried to take the stone back from her? With a sickening lurch she realised she could no longer feel her legs. Black smoke was twisting around her lower body, weaving and climbing. Her stomach prickled and turned numb. Her heart beat like crazy. An icy fist seemed to squeeze her chest until she couldn't feel it any more.

The Shadow leaned in close, took the Sparkstone from her stiffening fingers and hid it under his cloak. "Goodbye, Tainted girl." His hood was so close that for a second she caught a tiny glimpse of a thin mouth and pointed chin. The sight of his face made her shudder. Who was he and how did he seem to know so much about her?

He turned, his cloak swirling. Then he blasted red lightning at the hole to widen the tunnel. Sweeping through, he released another battering of lightning and the passage crumbled behind him, leaving the way out blocked by a heap of pale rock.

Laney remained frozen, unable to drop the arm that was stretched out in front of her. Her hand felt so empty without the Sparkstone. She moved her eyes to look at Tyler, motionless on the other side of the cave. He seemed smaller than before with his curly black hair flopping over his face.

She kept her eyes fixed on him as the black smoke swirled up to her neck. Then her vision glazed over and her lips turned numb and finally everything went black.

CHAPTER 15

When Laney came back round she was still frozen in the same position, her hand lifted in the air. The loss of the Sparkstone hit her immediately. Not only was it gone, but the Shadow had worked some kind of spell to smother its power. He'd said he was destroying all Blaze magic. Was he really strong enough to do that?

She could move her shoulders and head now, which meant the effect of the black smoke must be wearing off. Her arms and legs were still numb. She took a deep breath to calm her panic but a sudden noise made her heart jump. Tyler was digging at the pile of broken rock on the other side of the cave where the entrance used to be.

"Tyler," she called weakly.

"You're awake!" He came over to her. "I don't know how long I was out for. I came round a while ago and I've been waiting for you to open your eyes."

"I still can't move."

"My arms and legs took a while to come back to life too." Tyler touched her arm but she couldn't feel it.

"He took the Sparkstone," Laney said miserably.

The faint phosphorescent light from the cave roof glinted on Tyler's glasses. "It isn't over. We're going to get it back and make him pay." He went back to the pile of rocks and carried on pulling stones away from the rubble.

Laney's body tingled as it returned to life. "We have to shout for help. The others that were frozen by Shadow magic ought to be free now too. They might be able to dig us out."

"Good plan." Tyler cupped his hands to his mouth. "Hello! Anyone? Dad?"

"Uncle? We're in here!" Laney joined in.

They yelled for a while and then stopped to listen. There was no sound beyond the caved-in wall.

Laney opened her hands to make fire, thinking that more light would help, but no flame appeared. "My fire's gone," she said.

Tyler tried to make fire too. When he couldn't, he sat down on the cave floor and sank his head in his hands. "Our magic's gone! He's destroyed the Sparkstone."

"Maybe his spell will only last a little while. Maybe it'll wear off like the one that froze us into statues." Laney pulled at the crumbled rock, her fingernails full of dirt. Suddenly the cave felt small and stuffy. "Help me, can't you?"

Tyler started digging again in silence.

A moment later there were voices on the other side of the wall and a thumping sound started up.

"We're in here!" Laney shouted.

"We know! Stand back a minute – we're coming through," Claudia called back.

The thumping accelerated, shaking the whole cavern. Then a metal spade punched through, showering earth and rock across the ground. It burst through again, forcing a hole into the cave wall.

Tyler began pulling the larger boulders out of the way. Then he stopped short. "Oh, it's you!"

The man holding the spade peered through. "Yeah, it's me," said Chips Delaney. "She found me and said you needed rescuing." He glanced at Claudia before carrying on digging.

Claudia waited behind him, brushing the dust off her clothes. "Dizzy found him, actually. He was the only one out on the hillside."

"Not the only one in the air though," Delaney said grimly and Claudia shivered. He finished digging and stepped back to let them through the hole. "There. That should be big enough for you to get through."

Laney climbed through first. "The Shadow has the Sparkstone," she told Claudia and Delaney. "We have to find out where he's gone."

"We're defenceless like this," Tyler snapped. "We can't run around chasing the Shadow with no powers at all. We have to find Hillburn. He's the Elder."

"Our Blaze powers are gone," Laney explained to the others. "They disappeared when the Shadow took the Sparkstone."

Delaney rested on his spade, a look of pity on his face. "It's daylight. I can't believe the Shadow will want to be seen in the open so I suggest we get out of the tunnels. I think I can still remember the way out."

"Good, I've had enough of this place. It's creepy." Claudia wrapped her arms round herself.

Delaney led them through the dark tunnels, lighting the way with his torch. There were no statue-like figures against the walls this time. Laney was glad that the others had also broken free, but she felt the hairs rise on the back of her neck at the thought of what the Shadow had done.

Climbing up a steep tunnel, they reached the surface and scrambled past a bush that hid the cave entrance. Laney came out last, blinking in the cold morning light. She scanned the grey sky and was relieved to find that the red moon had set. She never wanted to see that kind of moon again. She went to follow the others when she noticed that the leaves on the bush had shrivelled and turned brown.

"What is it?" Tyler asked, noticing her expression.

Claudia answered for her. "If the Shadow gets close to a plant, it turns brown and dies. It must be the effect of his magic or maybe it happens when he's just finished a spell. I guess he must have come this way."

Laney hurried past the wilted plant and they walked down the hill in silence. Dizzy joined them as they followed the road into the village. When they got to the first row of houses, Delaney stopped.

"Aren't you coming to the bakery to find the Elder?" Laney said.

"Am I following you into Blaze headquarters? No, I don't think so." Delaney's mouth twisted. "I think I'll head home."

"Thanks for digging us out." Laney couldn't think what else to do, so she held out her hand and he shook it briefly before turning away.

"I ran into him at the bottom of the hill. He said he was wondering what was going on with the red moon," Claudia said quietly as they walked on. "He fetched his spade as soon as I said you needed help, though I think he partly brought it to use as a weapon against the Shadow. Your cousin doesn't like him, does he?" She nodded her head at Tyler, who was walking ahead of them.

"Lots of the Blazes don't like Mr Delaney. His parents were from different tribes and he fell out with them all years ago."

The bakery door opened a crack as Tyler approached and he slipped through the narrow opening. The door shut again.

"I don't think I should go in there," Laney said.

"Not after last night. Tyler will tell the Blazes what's happened."

Dizzy mewed and Claudia nodded. "We're going to the nearest Greytail house. I can ring my aunt from there," she told Laney. "Don't go looking for the Shadow, OK?"

"I've got to help!" Laney said. "I was the one that gave him the Sparkstone."

"Only because you had no choice, right?" Claudia replied. "This isn't your fault and you're helpless without Blaze powers."

Laney watched Claudia and Dizzy cross the street and turn down the road with all the Greytail houses. Turning away from the bakery door, she walked back towards Pebblenook Cottage. She was exhausted. She didn't know what time it was but it had to be really early because there was no one else about. If she turned up now Kim would know something was wrong and she'd want to know what had happened. She didn't think she could face lying to Kim again.

The curtains were drawn at the cottage windows so Laney went into the field next door and climbed on to the gate to wait for a while. She opened her hands and concentrated on making a flame appear. She did it the way Tyler had taught her – finding the fire in the pit of her stomach – but nothing happened. Could a Shadow spell erase her magic just like that?

She touched the round red mark on her middle finger where she'd been burnt that first time. Her dawn mark. What would the Blaze tribe do? Were they getting ready to take on the Shadow? She knew they wouldn't share their plan with her. They hadn't told her that they had the Sparkstone all this time.

She breathed in the cold air. Rainwater from last night had collected on the gate hinges like round glass beads. She touched a drop and it stuck to her finger. How was she doing that? Wasn't all of her magic gone?

"Laney!" Tyler sprinted down the street. "I didn't realise you weren't there till just now. I told the Elder what happened in the cave but he already knew the Sparkstone had been taken – he sensed it straightaway – and none of us have any power." He leaned against the gatepost, panting for breath.

"We have to get the Sparkstone back before things get even worse," Laney said. "The Shadow will have a plan for the Myrical. He always does."

"We have a plan too – but it won't be easy," Tyler told her.

Something glinted at the corner of Laney's eye.

The water drop lifted slowly from her finger and hung glistening in the air. Then, one by one, the other beads of water on the gate lifted too. They joined together making a little transparent ball that hovered, unblinking, almost as if it was waiting for instructions.

"Are you doing that?" Tyler's voice rose in disbelief. "You've been using Blaze power all this time, so how can you move water as well? No one has more than one kind of magic."

Laney flushed. "I don't know what's happening!"

"But it's you doing it, isn't it? So what *are* you?" Tyler stared accusingly at her. "I don't understand you!"

"I don't understand what's happening either but I'm trying to work it out. Please don't tell anyone!"

Tyler looked at her for a moment. "I won't. But this is really weird, Laney." He broke off, frowning. "I've got to go. I'll see you later." And he ran off down the road.

Laney let herself into the cottage as quietly as she could. The clock in the kitchen told her it was six thirty in the morning. She managed to creep upstairs without waking Kim or Toby and then she collapsed on her bed and kicked off her shoes.

She was a Tainted. Worse – she'd had two different kinds of magic, until the Shadow had destroyed one. But having two kinds of magic at the same time wasn't possible even for children of mixed-tribe parents. Maybe there was something strange about her just like the red moon prophecy said:

Born under a Wolf Moon
The Child of Aether joins together powers far
apart...

Well, if she was some Child of Aether it hadn't helped much when she faced the Shadow last night. She used to have fire and water magic.

Now she only had water.

When Laney woke up later, she was still lying fully clothed on her bed. Kim had obviously been in because her shoes had been tidied away and the curtains had been drawn. She wasn't sure how long she'd slept.

She'd been dreaming and the pictures had been as bright as a flame. She'd drifted to a time when she was very small and they were living in the countryside – a place where a big hill rose up behind the garden. One night her mum wrapped her in a blanket, picked her up and ran out of the house. Lightning split the dark sky all around them. Her mum hid her in the river and the water kept her safe.

Then the dream had shifted.

She was playing on a rug, banging on a little drum, and there was another baby opposite, so similar to her it was like looking in a mirror. Then the image faded and she was alone on the rug again.

Laney shook back her hair and the last threads of the dream evaporated.

The light seeping through the curtains was a strange bluish-white. Pulling them back, she found that it was nighttime again and snow was falling heavily. Her chest tightened. It was May, which was a pretty odd time of year for snow. It was hard to look away from the drifting flakes with their relentless rhythm. Kim's car was already covered with snow. The apple tree branches were sagging under the extra weight, the spring blossom smothered by frozen whiteness.

Laney let the curtain fall. She knew too much about the power of the Myricals to think this was a coincidence. If this was a Shadow spell then what was it for?

She lay down again, overcome by tiredness.

When Laney woke again it was morning. It had stopped snowing and the landscape glittered like white icing. The second she sat up, Laney thought about the light of the Sparkstone going out and her head spun.

Kim was in the kitchen making scrambled eggs for Toby, stirring the mixture with a wooden spoon. "You'll be pleased to know that school's cancelled. All the roads are blocked because of this silly weather. Snow in May – it's crazy!" She studied Laney. "Are you OK? You didn't even stir yesterday. Did you stay up really late at Claudia's?"

"I just needed to catch up on sleep, I guess." Laney poured some juice for herself and Toby. "When did it start snowing?"

"Around lunchtime yesterday and it just went on and on. The weather people on TV are blaming a freak weather system that's come from the Arctic."

Laney nodded. Humans always found an

explanation for these things. It was amazing really.

"Snow!" Toby flung a crust in the air.

"Toby!" Kim picked it up from the floor. "He's been very excited about the snow. We played out in it yesterday while you were asleep." She smiled at Toby. "We went out in our wellies, didn't we?"

"Wellies!" Toby threw another bit of crust.

"Toby! That's enough." Kim took his plate away. Then she started dishing out the scrambled eggs. "So where did you *really* go the day before yesterday?"

Laney thought she hadn't heard right for a moment. "I went to Claudia's. I told you."

Kim handed her some eggs and then sat down opposite. "Yes, you told me. Now, do you want to tell me where you really went?"

Laney started slicing the toast to give herself some thinking time. Kim had noticed more than she realised. She couldn't explain about the faerie world but it was about time she told her stepmum about the Embers. "Look, I'm really sorry I didn't tell you before, but I found out that my mum came from here – I mean she grew up here in Little Shackle." Her cheeks flushed. "And her brother – my uncle – still lives here. I've met him and my aunt and my cousin."

"Oh, Laney, are you sure they're your uncle and aunt?" Kim said. "How did you find them?"

Laney explained how she'd met her uncle. She

talked about the Embers family and the repair shop, and how her aunt and uncle had welcomed her. She should've known that Kim would be fine about it and it was funny how carrying one less secret made her heart a little lighter.

"Once this snow melts I'd love to meet them. Your dad would want to see them too." Kim's face fell. "I'd hoped to go to the hospital today but I don't suppose they'll clear the snow off the village roads."

The light bulb flickered and went out. Kim pressed the switch but nothing happened. She sighed. "That means the electricity's off now too."

"Maybe I could go to the corner shop and get something to cheer us up," Laney said quickly. "Some cherry slices or something." She really wanted an excuse to walk into the village and find out what was going on.

"That's a nice idea!" Kim took some money out of her purse. "Cake would be good, and we need some milk and margarine."

"Chocolate," said Toby.

Laney had to borrow Kim's wellies to walk into the village as she'd left hers behind in Skellmore. As soon as she was out of the house she let herself think about the Shadow and the stolen Myrical. It hadn't seemed safe to think about those things around Kim and Toby. She felt like it would bring evil into the cottage somehow.

Deep snow covered everything, so deep it came up to the top of her wellies. A few thin flakes were still falling. Laney wondered again whether this was the Shadow's work. He could never have used the Sparkstone's power to create this snow – the stone held the essence of fire magic. But maybe he was trying to break the Myrical's power…

Yes that had to be it. He must be casting a spell of cold to get control of the stone.

Laney gathered a handful of snow from the garden wall and squeezed it between her bare fingers. She expected it to melt round the edges but it didn't. She pressed it between the palms of her hands. There was no fire in her with her Blaze power gone but the snow still should have melted a little. Maybe it wasn't just ordinary snow.

Suddenly the snow seemed more menacing, with a mind and purpose of its own. Laney stuck her hands in her pockets and hurried down the road. Snow was just made from frozen water and if she really had Mist power then she might be able to do things with it – make it move or float. But she didn't. If this was the Shadow's doing then there was no way she wanted to play with it.

There were plenty of people about in the village. A group of kids were making a snowman in someone's front garden. A few people were shovelling snow off the path but she couldn't see Tyler anywhere.

Keeping her head down, she slipped into the corner shop and nearly ran into the long queue that stretched back to the door. Chips Delaney, who was standing by the newspaper rack, glanced at her briefly.

Tyler was at the front. "Matches, please." He put down some coins on the counter and the shop owner handed him a matchbox.

"That's my last box, everyone," said the shop owner. "I've sold out and I don't have any lighters either." Grumbling broke out in the queue. "I'm sorry but I've sold a huge number of boxes since last night and that's all I have."

Laney realised that she recognised a lot of these people from the Kindling. Tyler reached her, pocketing the matches. "Come on," he muttered. "I need to talk to you."

"I can lend you matches," Delaney told the people in the queue. "I've got some boxes at home." There was silence and Delaney's mouth set in a straight line. He walked towards the door saying, "Well, it's up to you. You know where I am."

Tyler drew Laney down a side street. "This is a nightmare. We've never had to buy matches before but none of us can light fires without them. With the electricity off we need fire to keep us warm."

"Has anyone seen the Shadow since last night?" Laney asked.

"No." Tyler frowned and kicked at the snow.

Laney had to know if she could trust him. "Did you tell anyone about me and what happened with the water drops yesterday?"

He looked her straight in the eye. "No, I thought about telling my dad but I didn't. It's too confusing and I don't think our tribe can take anything else right now. I won't tell if you don't want me to."

"I think I need to figure out what's happening myself." Laney folded her arms against the cold. "So what does the tribe plan to do about the Sparkstone?"

Tyler lowered his voice. "Hillburn thinks it's still underground. There's a Blaze spell that stops the Myrical being taken out of the underground passages. It was set up years ago – like an enchanted barrier – and it hasn't been broken."

"So the Shadow left the tunnels without the stone?"

"He probably had no choice. That spell he used to overpower us wore off after a while and Hillburn and the others started searching the tunnels for him. Maybe they got close just as the Shadow tried to get the Sparkstone through the barrier spell."

"So he hid the stone and escaped?"

"Exactly. So now everyone's setting out to search

the tunnels. None of us have any Blaze magic so we'll have to take torches." Tyler rubbed his hands together. "Stay out of the way, OK? The Shadow obviously has something against you. Don't give him another chance to hurt you."

"I can't just do *nothing*. I have to help." Laney broke off as Briana, Zac and Callum ran round the corner, calling out to Tyler. They stopped when they saw Laney, and Briana said something to the others.

Laney was too far away to hear but she could guess what the other girl was saying. "They still blame me for the red moon. They don't trust me."

"Well, I do! And I know you were looking out for me in the cave yesterday. But you should go back home now or you'll get yourself killed." Tyler squeezed her arm and ran to join his friends.

They raced back to the High Street and disappeared inside the bakery before Laney could argue so she went back to the corner shop and bought some milk and some squashed-looking cherry slices before heading home. Walking back up the hill in the deep snow was hard work but all she could think of was the Shadow. She couldn't shake the feeling that the Blazes were missing something.

Crossing the bridge, she began climbing the last stretch up to the cottage. Maybe the Shadow would be at Beggar's Chasm by the faerie ring. She'd seen him close to a ring once before back in Skellmore. The rings were gateways to the Otherworld and perhaps all the energy pouring through them helped his Shadow spells. Maybe she should go up there and see if she was right.

When she rounded the corner, she saw Kim and Toby waiting outside the cottage. Spotting her, Kim started waving her arms.

Laney ran to meet them. "What is it?"

"There's been a phone call." Kim's voice sounded weird. "From the hospital."

"What?" Laney's throat tightened.

"Your dad's got worse, they say, and he's having trouble breathing. They want to know if we can come in to see him – just in case."

Laney didn't want to ask what *just in case* meant. "But how are we going to get there with all this snow?"

"Mrs McKee knows a farmer and he's going to drive the tractor through the snow with us following. Once we reach the main road the route to Kirkfield is supposed to be clear."

The faint roar of an engine came from the end of the lane. "Quickly, put the shopping inside," Kim said. "We're going right now."

The crawl behind the tractor to the main road was painfully slow. Toby babbled cheerfully to himself in the back seat and spun the wheels on his little toy car. But Kim was silent and Laney didn't speak either. She didn't know what to say.

The snowfall had been lighter in Kirkfield and the roads were clear. Kim parked next to the hospital and they went inside.

"Keep hold of Toby, could you?" Kim rushed away down the corridor. "I'm going to try to find a doctor who can tell us what's going on."

Laney took Toby's hand and stopped outside her dad's room. *He's having trouble breathing.* Kim's words went round and round in her head. She made herself push the door open.

"Laney!" Simon was standing by the window. "Are you OK?"

Laney let go of Toby's hand and walked to the bed. She felt as if she were in a dream – her dad lying there looking like a ghost with an oxygen mask over his mouth. The beeping monitor behind the bed sounded like a warning.

"I drove up here to see you all but the roads looked so grim that I didn't think I'd get through," Simon told her. "So I came here and found Robert like this."

"The hospital rang us and said we should come in. Kim's gone to find a doctor." Laney sat down in the chair next to the bed and took her dad's hand. Was this real? She leaned closer. As always, her dad's eyes were shut tight. Beneath the mask his breathing sounded hoarse.

Toby crouched down, pushing his little car along the floor.

Simon broke the silence. "I'm amazed you got through ... such terrible weather..."

Laney tried to swallow. "They said he was worse when they phoned. So we had to."

Simon pulled a chair to the other side of the bed. "It might not be as bad as it sounds – maybe it's best to wait and see what the doctors say. Sometimes people pick up an infection in hospital. He's always been a strong person though, so whatever it is he'll fight it off, I'm sure."

Laney didn't say anything. She knew Simon was trying to make her feel better but it was just words. She wanted her dad back. Not this pale person in an oxygen mask.

She wanted him to tell her to be careful about the tribes, to tell her not to practise magic in the house, to tell her not to stay out after dark. She wanted him to get cross with her and say that she didn't understand how much trouble she'd be in. She just wished he'd open his eyes.

The skin on his hand was as thin as tissue paper. There were purple bruises where the drip had been moved so many times. She let go of his fingers. Why wasn't he fighting this?

"Are you going to be OK?" Simon looked worried. "Shall I find Kim?"

Laney shook her head. She wished he'd stop trying to talk to her. Toby had abandoned his car and was fiddling with some flowers in a vase. He pulled a pink rose out of the water and shook it. Kim had brought the flowers the last time they were here, Laney remembered. They were the only bright thing in the room. Her eyes filled with tears.

"I'll go and find Kim." Simon pushed his chair back and made his way to the door.

"Snow!" Toby waved the flower at Simon as if it was a sword.

The petals slowly crinkled and turned brown. Simon stepped away but the flower carried on wilting, its stem bending right over. Toby waved the dead rose again, looking confused. A few brown petals fell to the floor.

Simon looked at Laney.

She met his gaze and a sick feeling rose inside her. There was only one person she knew who had that effect on living things. A faerie with magic so dark and rotten that his presence could turn leaves brown and make plants wilt.

That person was the Shadow.

CHAPTER
17

Simon's face smoothed over and the worried look vanished. His eyes glittered as if he was calculating whether Laney had figured out his secret.

Laney stared at the dead rose. There was no mistake. The flower had changed in an instant. In the silence, she heard Kim's voice in the corridor outside. Toby heard it too. He dropped the dead flower and rushed out of the door calling, "Mummy, me hungry."

Simon took a step towards the hospital bed and Laney leapt up. "Don't you dare come near him!" she hissed.

"Now, now! Calm down. How are you going to explain to Kim what you're yelling about? You can't tell her because she doesn't know what you are." A thin smile twisted the edges of his mouth.

Laney felt ice cold. "You did this to him ... and he was your friend." Looking at him standing there in his jeans and brown jacket, it was almost impossible to believe. Simon had been her dad's workmate for years. Yet there were little things – the tone of his voice and the way he stood – that now seemed horribly similar to the shadow.

Simon's smile deepened. "I was his friend for a reason – just not the reason he thought. I came to watch..." His fingers tightened into fists.

Those fingers... Laney had seen them covered in black gloves, letting loose a torrent of red lightning. When she'd fought against him to save the Wildwood Arrow, hadn't she thought ice had formed on her neck? She'd wondered then if the Shadow was a Mist faerie.

Her gaze snapped back to his face. "Where's the Sparkstone? You've hidden it in the tunnels underneath Groaning Tor, haven't you?"

"And if I told you, what would you do? All you had were some Tainted Blaze powers and now they're gone. You're nothing, just like your mother was nothing."

A tiny groan came from the bed.

"Dad?" Laney took his hand. His eyes were still closed and there was no sign of movement.

Simon moved forward too, leaning over the bed. He clamped one rigid hand on her dad's forehead and at once Mr Rivers' face tightened and veins stood out underneath his skin.

"No!" Laney grabbed Simon's arm and tried to pull him away. "Get off him!"

Simon eyes filled with darkness. First it covered the gold rings and then the rest of his eyeballs until all that was left were two black holes. His throat rippled and out of his mouth came the cold voice of the Shadow. "I have been keeping him weak for months despite your miserable herb parcels." He pushed Laney and she fell over. "The extra power has been very useful. I only need a little more to break that Blaze barrier spell and take control of the Sparkstone completely."

Laney's blood pounded in her ears. All this time Simon had been stealing her dad's power – keeping him helpless. "Why are you doing this?" she whispered.

Simon straightened, his black eyes fixed on her. "There are sacred rings all over this land being walked over and dug up and built on by *humans*." He broke off as if the word tasted rotten in his mouth. "It's time we took back our land – it was ours in the first place, long ago when the Fair Eyes were free. Your Elders are happy to hide and to pretend that we don't exist. I shall set us free."

"You're not setting anyone free! You're just taking things that belong to other tribes." Struggling up, she was about to launch herself at him when the door creaked.

Simon whipped his hand away from her dad's forehead and pretended to be leaning over the bed in concern as Kim and the doctor came in. He blinked and his eyes returned to normal.

"Laney, are you OK? I thought I heard shouting." Kim had Toby in her arms. "Things aren't as bad as I thought. It's just that your dad's condition seems very changeable."

The doctor went to the bed and examined the heart-rate monitor.

"It might be best if Laney goes outside," Simon said smoothly. "I think it's all been a bit too much."

Laney stared back at his thin face, hating him. "Just go."

"Laney!" said Kim.

"It's all right." Simon gave his usual pleasant laugh. "This is hard on everyone. I understand. Well, you've got my number if you need me." He made his way out. Even the way he twisted round to pull the door open reminded Laney of the Shadow.

Kim looked at Laney in confusion.

"Mrs Rivers?" the doctor said. "He's had another drop in his heart rate. I'm going to order a few tests. Nothing to worry about. But could I ask you to go to the waiting area for a while?"

"Of course." Kim set Toby down and bent over the bed to kiss Laney's dad on the cheek. She lingered there for a second but there was no change. His breathing under the mask sounded even more ragged than before.

Kim straightened and picked up Toby again. "Come on. Let's get you something to eat."

Laney followed them out, her head whirling. She had to make sure Simon was really gone. "I'll catch up with you in a minute."

"What are you doing?" Kim looked worried. "Come to the canteen with us and have something to eat. Please."

"I won't be long." Laney dashed along the corridor and out of the hospital entrance, nearly skidding on a patch of trodden-down snow.

Just pulling away from the traffic lights was Simon's blue van. She watched it drive away, taking the turning towards Little Shackle. A flurry of snowflakes drifted downwards. People hurried past, trying to get into the warm. Laney's head ached. How had Simon lied to them for so long?

A wave of hopeless fury rolled over her and her legs trembled. Instinctively she opened her hand to see the flame – fire always came when she was angry – but there was nothing. Just the round red mark on her finger which had been there since the night she Awakened. What was she supposed to do now?

A nurse hurrying past said, "Are you all right, dear?"

Laney nodded dumbly and stumbled back into the hospital.

When she reached the canteen, she found Kim wiping her eyes with a tissue. There were three plates of sausages and chips and three polystyrene cups of water on the table. None of the plates of food had been touched. Toby was lying across the seats opposite, fast asleep.

Laney slipped into the seat beside her stepmum. She didn't think she'd ever seen Kim cry before, not even when her dad first got injured. "Sorry I ran out. Thanks for the chips." She picked one up and chewed it. It was hard to swallow.

"I know this has been an awful day," Kim began, "but we have to be there for each other. That's what your dad would want."

"I know." Laney tried to smile.

"The way you spoke to Simon just now ... we can't take things out on each other like that, OK?"

Laney pressed her lips together. Simon had really tricked them all. She'd never seen plants wilt around him before but maybe he'd been careful not to get close enough. Or maybe it only happened after he'd been using Shadow magic. He could be heading back to Little Shackle to perform more dark spells right now.

She searched her pockets. "Can I borrow your phone? I've left mine in the cottage."

Kim pulled her mobile out of her handbag but then put it straight back. "Actually my phone's run out of charge. Who are you trying to ring?"

Laney thought fast. She had to get hold of someone and tell them what she knew. She had no idea what Tyler's number was even if she had a phone that worked. "I have to go back to the village." She pushed her plate away.

"No, we're staying here and you have to talk to me. Stop shutting me out, Laney. I know I'm just your stepmum but we're still family and we've got this far." Toby stirred and Kim lowered her voice. "You have to tell me what's going on. I know there's something you're keeping secret. I'm not stupid!"

"I can't tell you!" Laney turned scarlet. "And I can't really explain why."

Kim looked at her for a while. "Please try. I promise I won't be angry no matter what it is."

Laney stared at the chips on her plate. The first thing she'd been taught after Awakening was never to reveal the faerie world. Humans believed they were a myth. She knew what Claudia or Tyler or Fletcher would say, but they didn't have a dad in a coma and a family split apart by Shadow magic.

Showing Kim would be easier than trying to explain everything. She glanced round. There was no one sitting close to them and their table was hidden from view by a pillar. There was a water drop clinging to the edge of her polystyrene cup and she touched it, moving it on to her finger. Then, very gently, she made the drop lift into the air and spin slowly. She touched another drop from the edge of Toby's cup and one from Kim's, and the three drops hung in the air, turning softly.

She could still hardly believe her Mist magic was working. She'd struggled for so long to use water spells that she'd been sure her powers were weak. Now they flowed from her fingertips.

Kim's eyes stretched wide. "How are you doing that?"

"I'm different from you." Laney let the water drops fall to the table. "I can do things with water and fire." She didn't add that her powers over flame were broken. "And I'm not the only one that's different. There are lots of us."

Kim swallowed and clasped her hands together tightly. There was a long pause before she managed to say, "Your dad's involved too, isn't he? I knew there was something strange going on and both of you knew about it. All the things that happened in Skellmore – the lightning, the flood... It's why he got hurt, isn't it?"

"Yeah." Laney bit her lip. "I'm sorry I didn't tell you before. I wasn't allowed."

"It seems impossible ... but it's true," Kim said to herself.

"I have to warn people in Little Shackle that they're in danger."

"Like your uncle – your mum's family?" Kim said. "There's more you're not telling me, isn't there?"

"Please let me go back there. I have to help them." Laney pushed her hair out of her face. "It might help Dad too."

Kim stared at the drops of water on the table. Then she stood up and gathered the sleeping Toby in her arms. "Right then, let's go."

Neither of them said much on the drive back to Little Shackle. The roadsides were still piled high with snow and it showed no sign of melting. The whiteness of the landscape began to hurt Laney's eyes.

Kim stopped outside their cottage. "I'll drop you here. I must go back to the hospital."

"Thanks." Laney started to get out but Kim stopped her.

"I never knew your mum. You and your dad had been on your own for a while when I met him. But I think I see her in you sometimes when you do things your dad would never dream of, and I think I know what she'd say if she was here right now. If there's danger, don't be a hero and don't be brave. Just hide, OK? Toby and I don't want to lose you."

Laney swallowed. "I won't do anything stupid. I promise."

Kim managed a smile. "I'm going to the hospital to stay with your dad. I'll be back tonight."

"Kim?" Laney held her gaze. "If Simon comes back, don't let him near my dad. It's really important. I'll explain later."

Kim's fingers tightened on the steering wheel. "All right, I won't."

Laney stood back and watched Kim turn round and drive back towards Kirkfield. Then she ran down the icy path to the village.

CHAPTER

18

Laney banged on her uncle's door, the bakery door and the door of any other Blaze house she could find, but there was no answer. Either they weren't opening the door to her or they were still searching the tunnels for the Sparkstone.

Where would the Shadow be? She stopped by the corner shop and a small black cat brushed against her ankles. Laney was glad to see Dizzy. "Where's Claudia?"

Dizzy mewed and set off down a side street leading to the edge of town. Laney followed. They were heading up the slope that led to Beggar's Chasm, she realised. The snow was even deeper here, but it had a frozen crust that let the cat pad lightly over the top. Taking the track that curved round the side of the hill, they entered Beggar's Chasm. The stream that usually gushed through the valley was covered with a thick layer of frost.

Laney shrank back against the canyon wall, her heart racing. A whirling mass of snow hung at the centre of the valley like a gigantic spinning snow globe. Shards of ice flew off. Some were caught by the faerie ring close by and vanished into the vortex.

A tortoiseshell cat crouched beside a boulder up ahead. It had to be Claudia in her animal form. "Stay here, Dizzy." Laney ran along the valley and ducked behind the rock. "Claudia, is that you?"

With a slow shimmering, the cat's limbs lengthened and its fur faded. At last Claudia crouched in front of her. "I saw the Shadow near that big white peak on the other side of the village. He must have disappeared into the caves for a while and when he came out again he flew off in this direction. He'd gone by the time I got here but I think he's in the centre of that snow storm." Her amber eyes fixed on Laney. "This is going to be a shock – I know who he is. I saw him transform."

"I know as well." Laney's fingers clenched. "It's my dad's friend, Simon Morden. I found out at the hospital."

"It's unbelievable!" Claudia paused. "Are you OK?"

Laney nodded. "If he went to Groaning Tor first, he must have collected the Sparkstone from where he hid it underground. But why didn't the Blaze Elders stop him?"

"I was too far away to see everything but he aimed lightning bolts at the ground in several places. I think he might have sealed some of the holes to the tunnels, trapping the Blazes underground."

Laney's skin prickled. She could imagine how horrible it would be to be trapped down there. At least they should be able to find another way out, eventually. There were so many cave entrances on those hills. "I wish we could go back for them but we have to stop the Shadow before he works out how to steal the Sparkstone's power. Imagine the Shadow with all the fire magic in the world."

Claudia shuddered. "He could destroy everything. But how do we stop him? We're not strong enough."

"Maybe if one of us distracts him the other one can take the Myrical back. I can't think of anything better."

Together, they darted along the chasm, hiding behind the rocks that were scattered over the valley floor. After a few minutes, they were close enough to feel the fragments of ice flying off the massive circle of whirling snow.

A dark figure burst from the centre of the sphere. Stretching his wings like a hideous bat, he sent a bolt of red lightning into the sky and whitish-grey snow clouds began to churn overhead. Laney felt the bitter cold stinging her face and fingers as the temperature dropped far below freezing.

"What's he doing?" Claudia hissed.

"He must be trying to overcome the fire within the Sparkstone," Laney whispered. "But look – his hands are empty and that means the Sparkstone must be inside that snow storm."

A moment later, the water gushing over the cliff into the waterfall started to freeze. The pool turned stiff first then frost formed all the way up until the cascade was solid ice. Jagged ice fingers stuck out where the water had spurted over the rocks.

"I have a bad feeling about this. He obviously doesn't care who sees him." Claudia wrapped her arms round herself and shivered. "This cold is easier to stand when you have fur." She shimmered and became the tortoiseshell cat again.

Clambering through the snow, Laney kept her eyes fixed on the Shadow, who was pacing up and down beside the whirling globe of ice. Claudia padded behind, her amber eyes watchful and her tail flicking from side to side. Laney wished she could change into a cat too. Not just because fur would be warmer, but to make herself smaller against the bare white valley.

The Shadow continued pacing, his black cloak flying out in the icy wind. What was he waiting for? Was the Sparkstone definitely inside that ball of spinning snow? Laney forgot to keep an eye on where she was treading. Skidding on a slippery patch, she slammed into a boulder.

The Shadow whirled round. "Who's there?" he yelled. "Show yourself or I'll strike you down."

Laney crouched low. She was hidden from view by a rock. Icy cold began to seep through her coat and jeans. Kim's words about being careful echoed in her head. Claudia was tensed beside her, as if ready to spring.

The Shadow glared round the narrow valley,

before sending another bolt of red lightning into the air. It formed two crooked prongs like a snake's tongue. The Shadow quickly stepped back inside the whirling globe of ice and vanished.

High in the sky, the snow clouds churned and a blizzard of flakes whirled downwards. As each snowflake hit the ground, it grew four legs and a tail. Sharp little teeth grew in the creatures' mouths and their wicked eyes glowed red. The snow rats came racing along the valley, shrieking. They bit the rocks and they bit each other. Then they spied Laney and threw themselves at her in a torrent of teeth.

Claudia pounced on the nearest rat. With a swipe of her claws, she sliced it in half and the rat crumpled until it was just a pile of powdered snow. Another wave of snow fell and more snow rats swept down the canyon. They climbed Laney's legs and bit her skin with icy teeth. She tore them off and threw them down. Each one shattered as it hit the ground, but more of the creatures leapt on to her.

Claudia sprang at the rats, breaking them to nothing. Laney's skin crawled from the feel of their horrible tiny feet. At last the rats stopped coming. Silently, Laney and Claudia crept closer to the whirling mass of snow hovering close to the faerie ring. Laney peered through the blizzard but it was too thick to see the Shadow inside. He must be casting dark spells over the Sparkstone.

Red lightning shot into the sky again. Then snow poured to the ground and grew into a huge vertical sheet of ice. The wall of ice grew, stretching into a gigantic barrier around the faerie ring and shutting off their view of the whirling globe of snow completely. Laney ran to the ice wall and pushed it hard. It was thick and tall, and there was no way to get through it. She clenched her hands. If she still had Blaze power she'd have tried to melt this wall.

Claudia shimmered and changed back into a girl. "We should just transform and fly over this."

Laney rested her fingers against the ice. "I don't know. Don't you think he'll have thought of that?"

"What else can we do? We'll never break through this wall."

Laney shivered. "I don't think it's a good idea. He'll spot us more easily in the air."

Claudia changed to faerie form. Flexing her amber wings, she lifted into the air. "That's why we have to be fast. Come on."

"Claudia, stop!" Laney saw the ice forming on Claudia's wings. Frost ran over them in a river-like pattern. Claudia tried to land but her wings wouldn't move and she lost control, vanishing as she fell behind the wall of ice.

"Claudia?" Laney hissed. "Are you all right?"

There was silence.

"Claudia! Can you hear me?" Laney bashed on the ice until her arms hurt. Then she leaned against it, trying to catch her breath. Beyond this ice wall, the Shadow would be using stolen magic – her dad's magic – to attack the Sparkstone. He'd almost killed her dad by stealing his power. She had to stop him. But first she had to get Claudia out, before the cold weakened her friend even more.

She followed the ice wall, running her hand along it. Maybe there was a crack somewhere, a chink where the barrier was thinner. She'd almost gone the whole way round before she found it. Putting her fingertips inside the crack, she wished she had her Blaze magic to melt the ice. What else could she do to break this wall?

A sudden thought made her heart jump. She didn't have Blaze powers, but she still seemed to have water magic. In fact, her Mist powers seemed stronger now that her fire magic was gone. Maybe she could summon water to force the crack open.

Gathering all her strength, she cupped her hands and wished for rain. Only a few drops fell from the sky, pattering on to her fingers. Whispering to the water drops, she sent them floating into the gap in the ice wall. When enough water had collected there she willed it to burst outwards. With a snapping sound, the chink widened and the crack ran further along the wall. Laney did the same again and again, until the gap was wide enough. Then she edged through, only to be faced with another wall.

Laney stumbled along the narrow corridor with towering walls of ice on either side. She turned a corner and then another, sometimes discovering new passages of ice and sometimes finding a dead end. Claudia must be trapped here but there was still no sign of her.

"Claudia?" she called softly, and heard an answering groan a little way ahead.

She crossed the maze, taking dozens of different turns. At last she found Claudia slumped against an ice wall, her teeth chattering.

"If I had any Blaze magic left I could make you warmer." Laney crouched down by her friend. "Can you change back to a cat? Like you said before – you'll be warmer."

"So … so … cold," Claudia said, but she didn't manage to change her shape.

"Stay here, OK?" Laney told her. "I'll come back for you."

The cold grew stronger as she made her way through the maze. The ice walls thickened, making the path narrower. Laney rubbed her cold hands. If another wave of snow rats appeared, she didn't know if she could fight them all. She had so little energy left.

"Toby and I don't want to lose you," Kim had said. They needed her and she needed her Blaze fire back. There were no cracks in the wall where she could force a gap. Maybe she could fly for just long enough to get over the next wall. But she must be close to the Shadow now.

Nearly out of ideas, she built a mound of snow next to the wall, piling more and more on to it. Then she scrambled up and used the mound to climb to the top of the wall. Her heart plunged as she stared over the top.

The whirling mass of snow had vanished. The Shadow was only a few steps away. He was holding his black-gloved hands above the Sparkstone as if warming them over a fire. His black cloak billowed out behind him in the frozen wind.

CHAPTER
19

Trembling, Laney slid down from the wall. She hated looking at the Shadow, especially now she knew who he was. Simon wasn't just *Simon* any more. He was someone cold and cruel – someone who'd befriended her dad for dark reasons. What was it he'd said? *I came to watch...* What had he meant? Why had he been watching?

She shuddered as a wave of icy cold crept over her. Whatever Shadow spell he was casting, it was strong. As she crept closer, a magpie flew down and landed on the snow. It looked at the Shadow and then at Laney.

The Shadow had lain the Sparkstone on a slab of ice and he was bent over it, muttering. His hood hung low, covering his face. Red lightning sparked from his fingertips, hitting the stone time after time. Laney crept forwards a little more. She was only a few steps away now, too scared to even breathe in case he heard her.

The magpie tilted its black-and-white head, watching Laney with beady eyes. Suddenly she wondered if this was the same magpie she'd seen in the garden and on the roof of Pebblenook Cottage. She'd seen a magpie outside her dad's hospital room too. The bird had a particular way of staring at her, as if it was waiting and thinking. It gave a sharp cry. *One for sorrow*, thought Laney.

The Shadow took something small from under

the folds of his cloak. Laney recognised the purse that Mrs Willowby had used to keep her husband's dust in after he died. A sick feeling surged from her stomach to her throat. He must have kept some faerie dust back when he cast that red moon spell on the night of the Kindling.

Now she was closer, she could see that the Sparkstone had changed. The smoky-grey crystal looked dull and there was no glimpse of a fiery heart at the centre. Was there much Blaze power left inside the Myrical? The burn mark on Laney's finger prickled. There *was* still some magic there. She could feel it.

The magpie cried out again. Then, to Laney's horror, it flew up to settle on the Shadow's shoulder. Laney could hardly breathe. Had the magpie been Simon's helper all this time?

Sweeping to his feet, the Shadow reached out and seized her arm. "You should not have come, Laney. You see, Vull has been keeping an eye on you for me so I know everything you've been up to." He glanced at the magpie, which gave a harsh cry. "This is the last time you will ever interfere in my spells! From the night you Awakened you have been blundering into my enchantments and ruining my plans."

Laney gasped. "The red moon on the night I Awakened – that was you!"

"I was casting a spell to look for Myricals." The

Shadow's grasp tightened, his fingers digging into her arm. "All I found was a Tainted girl. You should have died as a baby, just like the other one."

"Let me go!" Laney tried to struggle out of his grip. What had he meant – what other one?

The magpie flew down to settle on an icy boulder. The Shadow dropped the purse of dust and seized Laney's other arm. "Now you're here – I can think of a use for you after all." He let go of her arm and clamped one hand to her forehead. "I need a little more power. Let's see if any remains in you!"

Pain burst through Laney's forehead like a jagged icicle. She cried out and kicked the Shadow as hard as she could. He staggered and released her. From the corner of her eye, Laney saw a tortoiseshell cat slip behind a rock. Claudia had broken out of the maze and transformed.

"You're going to regret that!" The Shadow's hood slipped back. Simon's thin face was contorted with fury, his eyes completely black.

Laney's head throbbed as she backed away. "Why did you pretend to be friends with us? What did you want with my dad and Kim?"

Simon laughed coldly. "It wasn't them. They mean nothing to me. I was watching you." Laney's stomach plunged and Simon laughed again as he saw the look on her face. "Haven't you worked it out yet? You're different from the others."

Laney shook her head. "You're lying again! That's all you do – just lie to people!"

"Ask your father then." Simon pulled the hood back over his face and advanced on her. "Ask him what he's been hiding all these years."

The mention of her dad made Laney's anger rise. She dodged round the Shadow. He tried to grab her but the tortoiseshell cat ripped her claws across his ankle. Laney made a dive for the Sparkstone and was surprised at how cold and heavy it felt in her hand. Whirling round, she raced along the chasm. Her breath came in icy gasps. She had to get the Myrical out of here.

The Shadow fired a torrent of lightning, hitting Laney in the back. Pain like a knife seared through her skin and she landed face down in the snow, not far from the faerie ring. She gulped, waiting for the agony to pass, and her fingers tightened round the Sparkstone. Lifting her head, she watched the tortoiseshell cat take the purse of dust between her teeth and bolt down the hill. The magpie gave a loud cry and flew after Claudia in a flash of black-and-white feathers.

Struggling to her feet, Laney grimaced. Her back stung where the lightning had struck her.

The Shadow marched over and seized her wrist. "You should join me, Tainted girl! We'll open the faerie ring together. This Myrical contains the essence of all Blaze power and will give me more power than the Crystal Mirror or that Thorn Arrow. I shall use it to wipe this whole place clean of human vermin and the magic of the faerie ring will help me!"

Laney's eyes flicked to the faerie ring nearby. Already she could hear the faint singing drifting from the world beyond. "You can't do that! All those people – they're not really different from us!" She thought of Kim and Toby.

"Give it to me!" He tried to grab the Sparkstone but Laney stepped back. She could feel the fierce pull of the ring behind her.

"You can't have it!" she yelled. "I bet you can't work your spell without it."

The Shadow's hood flapped and Simon's thin face was revealed. "If you get caught by the ring you'll never come back!" He smiled nastily. "You'll get pulled into the Otherworld."

Laney swallowed and took a tiny step backwards. She could feel the tug of the ring growing stronger. A magical whirlpool of voices spun round her. "I don't care!" she said. "If it means everyone else will be safe then I'll do it." But she did care, she realised. She couldn't imagine never seeing Kim and Toby again … and not being able to speak to her dad one more time.

"Laney, be careful!" The voice came from inside

the ring. She knew that voice – she'd heard it before.

"Who are you?" Laney whispered.

The Shadow watched her carefully. "They say people can hear the voices of loved ones inside the rings. Can you hear your dead mother? Has she told you I was there the day she died? I was sent by the White Shadow to keep an eye on you – to work out why the curse hadn't killed you."

Laney shuddered. She didn't understand what curse he was talking about. "What did you do? Was it you that—" She broke off, unable to say the words.

"I never planned to kill her." The Shadow's gaze kept returning to the Sparkstone in Laney's hands. "It would never have come to that if she hadn't seen me and gone to raise the alarm."

Laney felt sick. She wasn't sure she wanted to know any more but she couldn't stop herself whispering, "What happened?"

The Shadow's mouth curved into a smile. "I had to do it. I struck her down with lightning and I would have taken her dust for my spells if your father hadn't stopped me."

Red-hot anger surged through Laney. "You monster!" She pointed her hand at the Shadow and a bolt of white lightning burst from her fingers. She dropped to her knees, shocked at herself. She hadn't even known she could make lightning.

The Shadow staggered backwards but quickly regained his balance. "Don't flatter yourself that your weak spells can affect me. I am a hundred times stronger than you and I could kill you a hundred times over. But if you give me the Sparkstone now, I'll let you live." He lunged forwards, his hand reaching for the stone.

"No!" Laney did the only thing left that she could think of. Whirling round, she flung the Sparkstone into the faerie ring. For one second, the Blaze Myrical twisted high into the air. Then the swirling currents of the ring caught it, spinning the stone round faster and faster. The singing from the Otherworld grew in a great crescendo, making the ice crack in the waterfall.

Then the Sparkstone tumbled into the centre of the ring and vanished.

Laney's heart went cold. The Blaze Myrical was lost and it was all because of her. But she'd had no choice.

The Shadow let out a terrible howl. "Cursed girl!" He marched over, grasping Laney by the throat. Ice crept over her neck, thickening on her skin. "This is the end for you – my lightning is the last thing you'll ever see." Thrusting her away, he stretched out his fingers.

Laney crumpled as the first bolt hit her in the stomach. She tried to scramble up but her legs wouldn't work. Lightning crackled again. She rolled sideways and the bolt grazed the arm of her coat.

Leaping up, she started running when a third bolt knocked her off balance. The pull of the faerie ring caught her and she fell into a pool of swirling mist. The ring dragged her down and the snow-covered valley disappeared.

"Laney!" called the voice from the ring. "Laney, hold on." A pale hand slipped into hers and a translucent face swam closer. At first it seemed like Laney's own face, but the girl's hair was so long and her eyes were a sharper blue. Her touch was soft, like holding on to a cobweb. The spinning had stopped but they were still sinking into the mist. A rippling transparent surface closed over Laney's head.

Simon's face peered down. His voice sounded faint. "Goodbye, Laney Rivers. No red moon prophecy could help you in the end." He turned away, the magpie fluttering on to his shoulder.

"I have to get back," Laney cried, but as soon as she let go of the pale girl's hands she was caught in the terrible swirling current again. The singing of the ring wove round her in a melody of many voices.

"Laney!" The pale girl took her hands again and the spinning slowed. "Keep hold of me. We can only do this right if we're together."

Laney stared at the strange girl who looked so much like her. "Who are you? I know you, don't I?"

"I'm Tara." The girl smiled. "I've been waiting for you – hoping you'd hear me from the other side. I'm your twin."

"My twin!" As soon as she said the words out loud Laney knew it was true. "It was you trying to talk to me all this time. How did you know who I was?"

"We're connected," Tara explained. "A magical curse killed me on the day we were born. But because of our close bond, my powers passed to you when I came here to the Otherworld."

"We're sisters!" Laney hugged Tara. It was like trying to hold on to a cloud.

Glancing round, she realised that they were still sinking. More and more transparent layers closed over their heads as they drifted slowly downwards. Laney's insides burst with joy at finding Tara but what about leaving Kim, Toby and her dad behind? She glanced up. There was nothing above but deep silence and a white vortex of snow.

"We don't have much time!" Tara said. "If the prophecy is true we may be able to restore magic to the Sparkstone and send it back – return it to the Blaze tribe where it belongs."

"The prophecy!" Laney's heart leapt. Could she

fix what she'd done – get the Sparkstone back to the Blazes? "Will it really help us?"

"I think so. In the Otherworld we know the songs of all the tribes. Sing with me!" Tara began to sing a song about fire. Laney copied her and voices all around them joined in. Laney began to see other faces in the mist – hundreds of them – each one a soul that had passed over to the other side.

The song grew fiercer and at last the Sparkstone floated from the depths and settled on Laney and Tara's joined hands. It was alight again, with a heart of glowing flame.

"My daughters." Laney's mum stepped out of the throng of figures and kissed Laney and Tara. "I'm so proud of you both. Take the stone back, Laney. Quickly, before the portal closes."

"But what about you?" Laney looked from her mum to Tara.

"We don't have the power to leave the Otherworld, but it's not your time to pass over," Laney's mum said urgently. "Go back – take the stone with you. Never forget that I love you."

They'd drifted so far down that the ripples had stopped. Not far below her feet, Laney could see a burning golden light. She had the feeling that if she passed through that light she wouldn't ever come back again. "I wish there was more time."

"You can always find us if you listen to the ring,"

her mum told her. "Picture yourself returning to the surface and we'll do the rest. Good luck, darling."

Laney tried to let go of Tara's hand to take the Sparkstone but a strange force seemed to hold them together.

"You have two powers – Blaze and Mist," cried a figure in the pale throng. "You can't take both powers back. You must choose."

Other spirits took up the cry. "You have to choose."

"How am I supposed to do that?" Laney asked.

"Go back to the beginning," Tara told her. "One of us was born with fire and the other with water. You just have to remember which one you are."

"I don't know!" Laney cried. "I can't remember that long ago. My powers didn't Awaken till I was twelve and then I got Mist powers first and then Blaze." The golden light was creeping closer. She could feel the heat from it warming her feet.

Tara released one of her hands and placed it on Laney's forehead. "Think back. Go back to the beginning."

Laney closed her eyes. Tara's hand felt soft on her skin like the touch of an ocean wave.

She was lying on a rug, a rattle in her hand. The crackle of fire in the grate. The tapping of rain on the window. She was longing for one sound. She was stretching out her fingers…

Which sound had she longed for? Who was she really?

The spirits swam in a circle, pushing her back through the rippling transparent layers. They sang of wind, rain and sunlight in a world they could never return to. Laney's heart ached at the wistful note in their voices. She felt herself spiralling upwards.

Blaze or Mist? She had to choose.

Laney opened her eyes as she burst out of the faerie ring and tumbled through the air. Holding the Sparkstone tight, she collapsed into the snow beside the frozen stream. Her hands grew warmer and warmer until flames burst from her palms. She stared at them, her stomach somersaulting. She'd chosen! She was a Blaze – just like her mum – and Tara was a Mist.

As Laney scrambled to her feet she saw the Shadow just in front of her, with his hood pulled low. Suddenly he twisted round and fired lightning across the chasm. Laney caught a glimpse of her uncle and other Blazes taking cover behind the boulders. There were more Blaze faeries at the top of the cliffs but none of them were close enough to help her.

"How did you do that?" the Shadow demanded. "No one returns from inside the ring."

Laney thought she caught a note of uncertainty in his voice. She had to make the most of his doubts if she was going to escape. "Have you forgotten the prophecy? Maybe I'm more powerful than you think I am." She hoped she sounded confident. Her fingers tightened around the warm Sparkstone.

"No, you can't be." The Shadow reached out to grab her but a tall figure leapt out from behind a fractured ice wall. Throwing himself at the Shadow, Chips Delaney yelled, "Run, Laney!"

Red lightning sizzled on the Shadow's fingers but Delaney pinned his arms down. Laney paused, shocked by Delaney's nerve, before she raced down the chasm. How could Delaney defend himself against a Shadow faerie? He didn't even have any magic.

Heart thudding, she stopped to look round. A lump came to her throat as she saw Chips Delaney lying still on the ground.

"Laney, how on earth did you appear from the ring?" Hillburn drew her into a hollow behind a piece of jutting cliff. "Is that…? You have the Sparkstone! The Shadow told us he'd destroyed the Myrical completely." Hillburn took the stone in his hand and tiny flames burst out all around it.

A shout came from the clifftops as other Blaze faeries discovered that their magic had returned. Lightning flickered through the air as the Blazes began firing on the Shadow.

Laney swallowed. "Please … I know you don't like him but Mr Delaney needs our help. He saved me."

"Don't worry," Hillburn said grimly. "The Shadow is going to be very sorry he ever took on the Blaze tribe. Stay here." He marched out into the snow.

White lightning zigzagged from the clifftop but it missed the Shadow. Blue lightning came from the other side, hitting the wall of the ice maze and cracking it in two. The Shadow swung round, firing red lightning at his attackers.

The chasm filled with Blazes leaping from the cliffs on outstretched wings. Lightning crisscrossed from all directions. Laney ran out, desperate to see if Delaney was all right.

The Blaze faeries raised their hands, pouring fire at their enemy. The flames gathered into a huge ball which engulfed the Shadow. His black wings began to shrivel. The Blazes advanced, their fire growing bright and savage. The heat made Laney step back. She shivered at the fierce determination in the eyes of the Blazes.

The Shadow collapsed on the ground, his hood falling back to reveal Simon's face. Lifting his arm, he tried to shoot another bolt but the red lightning died on his fingertips. At last he was still, his eyes completely black, staring up at the white-wisped sky.

A magpie flew down and pecked at his hood. Then, with a loud cry, it flew away. Gradually, a glow gathered around Simon's figure and, with a sudden flash of light, his body vanished, leaving a pile of grey dust in the snow.

"Mr Delaney, are you OK?" Laney rushed over to kneel beside the figure of Chips Delaney. His coat was torn and his shoulder slashed with deep red burns.

"I'm all right," he said faintly. "I just don't think I can move right now."

Tears came to Laney's eyes. "You shouldn't have done that. The Shadow could have killed you."

He smiled. "I couldn't let you be the hero by yourself, could I?"

Hillburn said urgently, "Laney, did the Sparkstone go inside the ring with you? This Myrical is full of new power." He held out the glowing stone. "Let Delaney hold it. Let us see if it can do anything for him. Quickly, before the moment passes."

Laney took the Sparkstone and placed it in Delaney's hand. Then she watched as an amber glow passed across the man's skin and the red welts on his shoulder knitted together. Laney held her breath as she watched the wounds heal. Delaney drew a deep breath and sat up. "That's amazing. I feel so much better already."

"Careful now, that's powerful magic," Hillburn told him. "You may be a bit dizzy."

Delaney handed the Sparkstone back to Hillburn. "I do feel a bit odd – energetic – like a bottle of lemonade that's been shaken up." He staggered upright and a flame burst out in the palm of his hand.

"Mr Delaney!" Laney gasped. "Look!"

Delaney stared at the fire he'd made. "I don't believe it! After all this time."

The other Blazes gathered round. Some of them smiled at Delaney awkwardly.

"How did this happen? All my magic was taken away years ago only a few days after my Awakening." Delaney didn't take his eyes off the flame.

"I think the Myrical drank in extra power inside the ring," Hillburn explained. "I felt it as soon as I touched it. I think it's time to start fresh, don't you?

Join our tribe again – with or without magic you have always been a Blaze."

Delaney met Hillburn's eyes. "Thank you."

Laney smiled. Turning, she found Tyler and Claudia at her side.

"What happened to you?" Tyler scanned her face. "They said you fell inside the ring but I was too far back to see."

"The Shadow struck me and that's when I fell inside," Laney said. "But the spirits helped me escape." She told them about Tara, her twin, and how her sister's magic had passed to her when Tara died. "It all makes sense now. I never understood why I had Mist and Blaze powers at the same time when everyone said that was impossible. I knew my dad had hidden the fact I was born on the night of a red moon and I thought there must be something wrong with me."

"Twin babies born to a Mist father and a Blaze mother," Hillburn said slowly. "One with water magic and the other with power over fire."

"So the prophecy really was about you after all, Laney." Claudia's eyes were wide. "How does it go? *Born under a Wolf Moon, the Child of Aether joins together powers far apart. She binds the opposites and drives a splinter through the faerie ring's heart.* But what's Aether?"

"No one really knows for sure," Hillburn said. "But

some stories say there is Aether in the Otherworld."

Laney thought of the strange mist inside the ring where the pale spirits lived. Had that been Aether? It was almost impossible to describe what it had been like in there. She saw the others looking at her curiously. "I'm just glad I got to meet Tara and see my mum again."

With a cracking sound, part of the ice wall behind them collapsed. Then a second crash echoed round the chasm as another part broke away.

"The cold is fading because the Shadow is gone." Hillburn held up the Sparkstone and everyone fell silent. "There's a lot to discuss but for now be joyful that our Sparkstone is back in our hands. We must not forget the ones who helped us." He nodded to Laney. "You have our deepest thanks, Laney Rivers, for saving our Sparkstone, and we must not forget the other young lady. The one who ran off with the dust the Shadow was trying to use. I have to say I never expected to owe such a debt of gratitude to a cat!" A ripple of laughter ran around the group.

Claudia smiled and tossed her long dark hair over her shoulder. "I ran back to the village and gave Mr Willowby's dust to Gwen Whitefern, the Thorn Elder. It'll be safe with her."

Hillburn lifted his arms. "Now, in this place far from human eyes, let's join together to share our fire magic." Each Blaze raised their hands and lit a golden flame. They burned strongly together, bright and tall and unwavering. Delaney joined in, the fire casting a glow across his face.

Laney slipped to the edge of the group. "I have to go. The hospital called my stepmum this morning because my dad had got worse. I have to go back to Kim and Toby." She ran along the chasm, through the deep snow.

Claudia caught up with her. "I'll ask my mum to give us a lift back to Kirkfield. She came here with the other Skellmore Elders when news of the Shadow and the Sparkstone got out. I saw them all in the village earlier but the Blaze tribe wouldn't let them on to the hills."

Laney's chest tightened. She remembered how awful her dad had looked after being hurt by Simon's shadow magic. She longed to see him well again. There was so much she wanted to say.

Mrs Lionhart drew into the hospital car park as daylight faded. Laney climbed out of the car. She was grateful that Claudia's mum hadn't bombarded them with too many questions about the Myrical and the Shadow. She wasn't sure she had the words to describe anything right now.

"Urgh! It's turning to slush," Claudia said, stepping out into the soft snow. "I didn't think it'd melt so fast."

Laney led the way towards the hospital entrance. Already the white blanket across the roofs and fences looked thinner, and water dripped slowly off the branches of the trees.

"I can hear Gwen and Lucas," said Mrs Lionhart. "Perhaps they came to see your father, Laney."

Laney knew she must be right – she was used to Greytails having a sharp sense of hearing and smell. But why had Gwen Whitefern and Frogley come to the hospital? A sudden wave of panic hit her and she dashed down the corridor and burst into her dad's room. "Dad? What's happening?"

Gwen was standing next to the hospital bed with her hand on Mr Rivers' forehead. Bunches of herbs were spread out around the edge of his pillow and they filled the room with a sweet scent. Her dad's eyes were closed and his face was calm as if he was dreaming peacefully. The oxygen mask was gone.

"It's all right, Laney," Gwen said. "He's over the worst, I'm sure of it." She picked up a sprig of dried flowers and rubbed them between her hands before placing them back on the pillow.

Frogley stood by the window, his mouth drawn into a thin line.

"You mean he's going to be all right now? He's going to get better?" Laney said eagerly.

"I believe dark magic was blocking his recovery and now it has lifted. I've done what I can to speed his healing. Come here and see for yourself." Gwen beckoned Laney to the bedside. Then she picked up her hat from the window sill. "Come, Lucas, we should let the Rivers family have some privacy."

"What if the nurses and the girl's human stepmother come in and see all these dried leaves?" Frogley demanded. "And what about this girl's secret Blaze power which was deliberately hidden from us while she lived in Skellmore? Did she learn the Shadow's identity before he was killed? There are many matters to clear up."

"Yes, but not yet," Gwen said firmly. "Some things are more important than tribe matters."

Frogley didn't look as if he agreed but he followed Gwen to the door. Claudia and Mrs Lionhart were waiting in the corridor outside.

Gwen turned. "Oh, Laney, I believe Kim will be back in a moment. We sent her to have a cup of tea. Just tell her the herbs are a hobby of mine – herbal medicine, perhaps. It's not so far from the truth."

"I will." Laney heard the door close but all she could do was gaze at her dad's face. His skin seemed brighter and the lines on his forehead a little smoother.

"Thank goodness you're here!" Kim came in carrying Toby. "How did you get back?"

"Claudia's mum brought me." Laney smiled at her stepmum. "The danger I rushed to warn everyone about has gone."

Kim sat down in the chair opposite and studied Laney. "I don't know what question to ask first, I've got so many. Did you put all these dried flowers here?"

"They're Gwen's."

Kim nodded thoughtfully. She looked as if she was going to ask something else. Then she sprang up. "Robert?"

Mr Rivers' eyelids flickered open.

Laney looked into her dad's gold-ringed eyes. "Hi, Dad."

"How are you feeling, Robert?" Kim scanned his face anxiously.

Robert Rivers looked from Laney to Kim and tried to speak but it came out as a croaking sound. Kim poured a cup of water and held it for him while he drank.

Laney's eyes welled up and she gave him a huge smile. "Don't talk yet if it's too hard."

Her dad tried again. "I feel like I've been dreaming." He pressed Laney's hand. "Sometimes I could hear you calling me but I couldn't reach you."

"You're back now," said Kim. "That's what's important."

"I'm back," said Robert Rivers. "And I'm never going away again."

CHAPTER 21

Robert Rivers was kept in hospital for the next few days so that the doctors could observe him. They couldn't work out why he'd suddenly recovered but every test they ordered showed that he was completely well and just needed to build up his strength again.

The third time they visited, Kim took Toby to the canteen to buy him a sandwich, leaving Laney and her dad alone.

"Laney? Come and sit down." Her dad gestured to a chair by the bed. "I know there are things you haven't told me." He watched eagerly as she sat beside him. His face was still pale but his cheeks had lost their hollow look.

Laney hesitated. "I didn't want to worry you with things. The danger's past now..."

Her dad placed his hand on hers. "The last thing I remember is facing the Shadow back in Skellmore. You have to tell me everything. Don't worry – I'm strong enough to hear it."

So Laney explained what had happened in Skellmore after he'd been taken to hospital, and everything she'd learned since arriving in Little Shackle. She told him how she'd discovered her own fire magic and how she'd first met her uncle, her aunt and Tyler. Her dad's face darkened as she spoke of Simon and the day he'd stolen the Sparkstone.

"Gwen Whitefern visited again yesterday and spoke to me about Simon," he said at last, his hand shaking a little as he lifted a cup of water. "I can't believe I was so blind. I put us all in danger."

"It wasn't your fault," Laney said quickly. "None of the Elders realised what he was either."

Mr Rivers stared out the window for a moment, his mouth drawn in a straight line. Then he sighed. "Poor Cordelia ... but she would have been so proud of you." He smiled at Laney. "She always said you were a fighter."

Laney's heart fluttered. Her dad hardly ever spoke to her about her mum like that. "But, dad – why didn't you tell me she was a Blaze and that I might be one too? And why didn't you tell me about Tara?"

Mr Rivers' eyes grew watery. "I'm sorry – I always meant to tell you one day but I wanted to wait until you were ready. I know I waited too long." He took a deep breath. "You see, your mum and I went into hiding after we were married – there was so much hatred among many faeries for couples from different tribes and I knew we were in danger. That's how I kept us safe – by keeping our lives a secret – and I really thought it was working until the day I brought the twelve baby gifts home."

Laney leaned forward, watching his face as he searched for the words.

"You weren't brought up as a faerie so you don't know all the traditions, but in the Mist tribe it's customary to give twelve gifts to a mother expecting a new baby. I made a trip back to my home village to collect gifts for your mum from my friends and relations. We expected you to be born any day. Cordelia was so excited when I got home with all the parcels." His face looked sad. "I went to make her a drink as she started opening the wrapping paper and by the time I came back she was lying on the floor, white as a sheet."

"What happened?"

Mr Rivers swallowed. "There weren't twelve gifts at all – there were thirteen. An extra gift was hidden inside one of the others. I can't remember how many times I've wished myself back to that moment – wished I'd checked them before I got home and then thrown the whole lot away." He met Laney's gaze. "The thirteenth gift was a curse, you see. I knew which one it was as soon as I saw it – just an empty gold box edged with tissue paper. Someone had used Shadow magic to put the curse inside and as soon as Cordelia opened the gift, it killed your sister."

Laney's heart went cold. "It must have been put there by Simon or the White Shadow he was working for," she whispered, remembering how Tara had said she'd been killed by dark magic.

"But they can't have known that you were twins and the curse wasn't strong enough to hurt both of you." Mr Rivers took a shaky breath. "You were both born that night. Tara was so silent and beautiful while you were full of life. None of us knew, then, that her powers had passed to you."

"She's still amazing," Laney told him. "She helped me survive when I fell into the ring."

Her dad's hand tightened on hers. "I nearly lost you. I'm so sorry I didn't tell you all this before."

Laney squeezed his hand back, smiling. "So no more banning candles and matches from the house?"

Her dad laughed. "That was silly of me. I knew the touch of fire could Awaken a Blaze faerie and I thought you'd be safer as a human. Now I know better – you're safer with strong magic of your own. Although maybe you should just practise Blaze spells outside the house. I'm sure Kim doesn't want scorch marks on the walls!"

Laney laughed and hugged him.

The following day, a Council of Elders convened in the room behind the village bakery with Alfred Hillburn, Gwen Whitefern, Mr Frogley and Mrs Lionhart. Laney was asked to attend and explain what had happened in Beggar's Chasm the day that Simon had died. Many of the Blazes came to listen, including Laney's uncle, aunt and Tyler, and Claudia came too. There was a lot of discussion about Simon's treachery and his efforts to master the Sparkstone.

Then Gwen recounted news from the Kestrel tribe in the north, who had been fighting a terrible White Shadow that had attempted to take their Myrical, the Vial of the Four Winds.

"The Myrical is safe for now, according to the Kestrel Elders," Gwen said seriously. "I shall travel north to meet them tomorrow and share the good news about the defeat of our Shadow. The tribes must work towards greater harmony. Quarrelling among ourselves only helps those who use this dark magic."

Even Frogley, the sour-faced Mist Elder, nodded in agreement.

"And I would like to congratulate Laney on joining the Blaze tribe," Gwen continued. "It was clear from the start that your magic was strong, my dear, and yet your Mist power never seemed to work. Now we know about your twin I can see why your magic was so tangled."

"We will hold a late Kindling ceremony on top of Groaning Tor tomorrow night," Hillburn announced. "This will complete the earlier celebration that was interrupted by the Shadow's red moon spell. Laney, we'd like you to complete the ceremony to join our tribe as you should have done that night. Faeries from other tribes are also welcome to attend."

Laney beamed. She was finally joining the Blaze tribe just like she'd always wanted. She turned to ask Claudia if she would come to the ceremony but her friend had slipped away.

At the end of the meeting, Laney's uncle stopped her as she left the bakery. "Do you have time for a walk? There's a place I want to show you."

Laney nodded, knowing that Kim wasn't expecting her till later. She followed her uncle along the road out of the village.

"I went to visit your dad yesterday," he told her. "It's good to see him looking so well."

"I know. The doctors are amazed at how fast he's recovering." Laney realised they were taking the track to Beggar's Chasm. Her uncle led them round the side of the rocky slope and past the cave that guarded the ravine's entrance. Jagged cliffs rose up on both sides of the narrow valley and crows circled overhead.

Suddenly Laney knew where they were going. "You're taking me to see where you buried my mum's dust, aren't you?"

"Yes, and I'll show your father too, once he's strong enough." Her uncle beckoned her to one side of the chasm where the waterfall cascaded down the cliff into a frothy pool. There, beside the water, was a small grassy mound with purple heather growing on it. The snow from a few days ago had completely melted away.

Mr Embers cleared his throat. "I put her here. I liked the thought of her becoming a part of the place she loved so much, and they say it's good for a faerie to be buried close to a ring."

Her uncle walked to the far end of the ravine to give her some time alone. Laney sat down by the mound thinking of her mum – the Blaze faerie who'd loved water – and her twin sister, Tara. Cupping her hands, Laney gathered some water from the pool below the waterfall and sprinkled it over the heather. Then she walked slowly towards the faerie ring.

As she got closer, haunting music made the hairs rise on the back of her neck. Leaning in, she said softly, "Mum? Tara? Can you hear me? Dad's been ill but he's better now and the Sparkstone is safe with the Blaze tribe again. I'm joining the tribe as a true member tonight."

Listening hard, she caught an echo of their voices as if they were calling from some valley far away. For a moment, she thought she glimpsed a pale face inside the ring. A girl that looked almost the same but with longer hair and lighter eyes. Her sister.

Returning to the pool beside the waterfall, Laney

picked a sprig of heather from the mound where her mother had been buried. She went back to the ring and dropped the flower, letting it catch in the swirling current. She promised herself she'd return soon.

There was a fluttering in Laney's stomach as she climbed the slope to Groaning Tor the following evening. Tyler chatted all the way about the Sparkstone and how he'd managed to hit the Shadow with a ball of flame. "I mean, I'm not saying it was what finally defeated him but it was a good shot, y'know. It hit him right on the chest. Bam!"

Laney grinned. With the Shadow gone the whole atmosphere around Little Shackle was different. Blaze faeries who'd only nodded to her before were stopping to say hello.

Strains of wild music drifted down the hillside and soft mist swirled round them as they made the final climb.

"Did Frogley make this mist?" Laney said, surprised.

"I heard he offered to do it to hide the celebrations from human eyes," Tyler replied. "Handy trick, huh? Maybe this new friendship between the tribes will really work."

When they reached the summit, Laney gazed

round with her heart racing. The hilltop was dotted with golden flames and the tallest one blazed from the peak of Groaning Tor itself. New arches of May blossom had been made and people were already leaping through them. Laney felt the music fill her with a wild energy and she wanted to throw herself into the dancing straightaway.

Tyler nudged her. "Claudia's waving at you."

Laney swung round and gasped. There was a tall boy beside Claudia with untidy brown hair. "Fletcher!" she yelled, rushing across the hillside and hugging him. "When did you get here? I didn't know you were coming!"

"Claudia rang me and told me I should come and watch you become a proper Blaze," Fletcher grinned. "My dad drove me here today."

"I'm so glad you came!" Laney smiled back. "This is my cousin, Tyler."

"Hi." Fletcher nodded at Tyler before turning to Laney. "I guess you've had a pretty exciting time here. You'll find it a bit dull coming back to Skellmore."

"Laney's staying with us in the summer holidays," Tyler put in. "And that's only a couple of months away so she won't be gone from Little Shackle for long."

Just then Alfred Hillburn called for silence. "Welcome, fellow Blazes, Mists, Greytails and

Thorns. We're here to complete our Kindling celebration and welcome new members to the tribe. Most of the ceremony has already been completed and there is only the final part to do. Laney, you shall go first!" He motioned her forwards. "Touch the flame burning at the top of the tor and you will become one of us."

Laney climbed over the rocks to reach the peak. Nervously, she stretched out her hand and touched the golden fire pouring from the crack in the hilltop. There was a flash of sparks and she felt as if the fire ran right through her. It was warm and full of energy. It made her feel as if she could do anything.

A round of applause broke out in the crowd. Laney's friends scrambled over the rocks to join her.

"You did it!" Tyler told her. "You're one of us now."

"Well done, flame girl," Fletcher said with a grin. "All that Blaze practice really paid off."

Claudia swept back her dark hair. "I don't like the frost flames though! I've had enough cold for one week after all that horrible snow."

"No frost flames – I promise!" Laney linked arms with Fletcher and Tyler as she watched the Kindling ceremony go on. Fiery sparks danced in the sky and the wild music grew faster and faster. Laney smiled. Here, on the pale peak with flames burning brightly all around her, she knew she'd never been so happy.

Acknowledgements

Firstly, I'd like to thank my editor, Sarah Levison. Sarah has worked on so many books with me and I would be lost without her insightful comments, her eye for detail and her unfailing good humour. She makes everything a thousand times easier and more fun! I'd also like to thank Nicola Theobald who designed the covers for this series, Sarah J. Coleman, who created the lettering and the maps, and Lisa Evans who illustrated the beautiful front covers.

I must thank my family for sharing the ups and downs of life as an author. It can't be easy living with someone who stares at the computer a lot of the time, occasionally breaking into bouts of fast typing as if their life depended on it!

Lastly, I'd like to thank my sister, to whom this book is dedicated. A few weeks before I began writing the story, we travelled to the Peak District and stayed at the Youth Hostel in Eyam. We spent the day walking from Baslow all the way along Curbar Edge and Froggatt Edge where great shelves of rock jut out above the valley. These places are the inspiration for Little Shackle, Groaning Tor and Beggar's Chasm. The Dark Peak is such an amazing landscape. I only wish I lived closer and could go there all the time.